THE SEASONS OF LOVE

Stephanie laughed off warnings of summer holiday love affairs. She was quite sure she could resist the famed beauty and passion of Greece, and concentrate on her new job as tour leader of a group of Australians. It isn't a handsome Greek who steals her heart, but an Englishman named William Brown. But is he who he says he is? And, more importantly for her, is it the wrong season for a long-lasting romance?

ZELMA FALKINER

THE SEASONS OF LOVE

Complete and Unabridged

LINFORD
Leicester

First published in Great Britain in 2007

First Linford Edition
published 2009

British Library CIP Data

Falkiner, Zelma.
  The seasons of love - -
  (Linford romance library)
  1. Tour guides (Persons)- -Greece- -Fiction.
  2. Love stories. 3. Large type books.
  I. Title II. Series
  823.9'2–dc22

  ISBN 978–1–84782–716–6

Published by
F. A. Thorpe (Publishing)
Anstey, Leicestershire

Set by Words & Graphics Ltd.
Anstey, Leicestershire
Printed and bound in Great Britain by
T. J. International Ltd., Padstow, Cornwall

This book is printed on acid-free paper

1

The purple suitcase with its discreet *Far Corners* luggage tag shuddered its way through the rubber strips at the far end of the creaking luggage carousel and began to inch toward Stephanie. She breathed a tiny sigh of relief; the first hurdle was cleared. She was in Athens and her clothes, carefully packed between layers of bubble-plastic, had arrived on the same flight with her.

That had been one of her worries on the long trip from Australia and the stopover in Dubai. Even now that it was safely over, nervousness fluttered through her at the thought of arriving in Greece with only a cabin-bag. It was daunting enough to be beginning a new job without that added hassle.

Excusing herself to the wall of broad backs, she wormed her way from the outer edges of the densely-packed crowd towards the carousel until only one man, already surrounded by a mound of luggage, remained in her way.

'Excuse me,' she begged politely.

The broad figure in Arab dress did not move as the conveyor belt brought her trolley-case closer. Determinedly, she tried to get around him, but found she was boxed in between his belongings, his luggage cart and the crowd of mostly men. All bigger than her.

The purple case was looming.

Stephanie tried again. 'Excuse me,' she repeated in a louder voice. Once again, the request was lost in the hub-bub of the busy baggage area. Behind her, an anxious somebody pushed their trolley into the back of her knees.

She shuffled sideways, feeling her skirt catch on the ragged edge of a large, immovable object. Too late now to wish she'd been less concerned about the heat and creating the right impression in Dubai and chosen to wear jeans that morning. A long, flowing skirt was unsuitable for the madhouse this had turned out to be.

Her trolley-case was right in front of her now. There was nothing else for it. If no-one was going to move, she had to. She made an awkward lunge over what seemed to be a whole household of goods, stretching out on tip-toe to grab at the handle.

It wasn't one of her better ideas. Even as her grip tightened, without the anchor of two feet firmly on the floor, she felt herself being dragged along in its wake.

The snagged skirt tugged sharply, then gave way, ripping free with an ominous sound. She sprawled across the pile of belongings, catching a glimpse of a startled African face as she went down.

She let go — she had to. Ahead, the purple case moved on to begin another slow circuit of the carousel, via the rubber-barrier and the recesses of the airport baggage handling facility. At least, that was what it should've done but, as she watched in dismay, an anonymous arm reached out from the tightly-packed line-up of passengers and lifted it off the conveyor belt.

'Wait, that's mine!' she shouted as she struggled to extricate herself from the bedding, boxes and other worldly possessions that surrounded the African man.

'Someone has taken my bag,' she explained. There was a flash of teeth but no understanding or help from him.

Getting out of the crowd around this particular carousel was even harder than making her way in had been. The next carousel had ground into action and no-one in that crowd was prepared to give an inch, either. Really desperate, Stephanie burrowed through the crush in the general direction of the bag-snatcher.

The only reassuring thing was the colour of her case meant she had no trouble following it, even without the *Far Corners* tag. That had been the idea in choosing purple. That, and the fact it

4

was a special price in the after-Xmas sales.

Thrown out of work because of the collapse of one of the country's major airlines and facing an unknown future job-wise, she hadn't wanted to spend a lot of money.

Once clear of the immediate pack, Stephanie looked around for an official. They would need to move quickly to alert Customs before the thief slipped through unchallenged. There was no sign of anyone of authority, not even a baggage-handler or a porter.

Swinging back in the direction of the carousel, she caught a glimpse of the purple trolley-case. Quickening her steps she was surprised to see it being pulled toward her, against the flow of passengers.

Her startled gaze went to the thief. He wasn't behaving the way she expected.

Perhaps that was his strategy, to appear unconcerned, part of the milling crowd until it carried him close to an exit.

Stephanie could see the man quite

plainly now. A head taller than many around him, he seemed to be searching, too. Did that mean he had an accomplice? How could she handle more than one? Where were Security?

There was no time to wonder, their paths had converged. It was now or never.

'Hey, that's my luggage!' she exclaimed indignantly, quite forgetting the years of training in diplomatic restraint as a flight attendant.

She made another lunge at the trolley-case. It was no better than her first attempt. She immediately realised she should have gathered herself before attempting to wrest it from the man. Off-balance, she teetered, then fell against his firm body.

It was like fronting up to a brick wall. A tangy-smelling brick wall, if such a thing were possible. Needing both hands to steady herself, Stephanie relinquished her hold on her case for the second time that day.

She let herself stay there, clinging to

the man, taking deep breaths and wondering what brand of aftershave he used. It reminded her of the outdoors, and fresh air, as far removed from where they were as she could imagine.

'Yes, I know it's your luggage,' replied a voice above her.

That brought her up with a start. She lifted her head from the stranger's chest and realised he had let go of the trolley-case, too. His arms were around her, not tightly, but firmly. Alarmed by their comfort, she backed out of their circle.

'You know?' she spluttered.

'Yes, I was at the next carousel, saw you were . . . er . . . having difficulties, and helped out.'

Stephanie gave him a searching look. Could she believe him? Or was he improvising now he'd been caught? It was hard to tell. The blue eyes that gazed back from out of the lightly-tanned face seemed guileless enough. In fact, the longer she looked at him the more reassured she became. This was no local, would-be thief.

Immaculately groomed despite having just come off a flight, the stylishly-cut fair hair that flopped across his forehead, the firm, clean-shaven chin and classic features singled him out in the seething crowd. Her experienced eye told her he was definitely a business-class traveller. Not someone needing to steal luggage.

She recovered some of her aplomb. 'Thank you for being so thoughtful,' she said in her best flight-attendant manner.

Suddenly conscious of his direct gaze, Stephanie straightened up, furtively tucked the loosened ends of her shirt back into the waistband of her skirt and instinctively put a hand up to her hair.

It was a wasted effort; her good samaritan showed no inclination to linger. Without another word, he nodded slightly and turned toward the Customs Hall. Well, it obviously wasn't a sophisticated pick-up routine, she decided.

Stephanie watched the tall figure stride through the thinning crowd, a suit-bag slung over his shoulder . . . A suit-bag? Her mind latched on to the fact he carried no heavier luggage.

What had he been doing waiting at the next carousel if there was nothing for him to claim? Was he in reality a thief, a very clever one? One she had thwarted?

She hadn't time to congratulate herself. After all, she would never get an answer anyway; he was gone. Right now she had to clear Customs herself and make a connection with Yanni in the Arrivals Hall as arranged. At the barrier she shrugged off her cabin back-pack for inspection, expecting to be waved through after a cursory glance.

Suddenly, she was surrounded by three Customs Officers, her case seized and swung up on to a bench.

'Open your bag!' ordered the unsmiling senior man.

Stephanie's first reaction was to protest, but was dissuaded by the stern look on his face. Welcome to Greece! The delay with her bag meant she was among the last of the passengers and the officers were looking for work. She produced her keys and opened her case to the probing fingers of Customs.

It didn't take long and Yanni still waited for her by the exit doors, a reassuring bulk of a man. He waved aside her apologies for the delay and directed her toward the taxi-rank, talking all the while as if it was only yesterday they last met.

'The travelling was good, yes?' Without giving her time to reply, he went on. 'Everything has been arranged. You are not nervous, are you? There is no need. Yanni will watch over you.'

'I am not nervous, Yanni,' she replied, knowing it was a lie she told herself, and now, him, to bolster her spirits. He was wrong; there was a need. Getting out of the airport hadn't exactly been a calming experience, but there was another reason to be nervous.

This was her first solo overseas trip

as Tour Director for the Far Corners Travel Company. On a run-through with the retiring director at the end of last season she'd felt confident, but now, six months later, faced with managing the tour on her own, little doubts rose to the surface.

The enjoyment and safety of fifteen people depended on her. No wonder there was a sinking feeling in the pit of her stomach.

'I know you will watch over me,' she added truthfully. That was his job. Hers was the welfare of the members of the group, to be their Australian contact in a delightful but unfamiliar Mediterranean country.

She and Yanni talked details on the way into the city. It took Stephanie's mind off the horrendous traffic that defied description.

Even though the Olympics had resulted in an improved road system, to her eyes it seemed chaotic.

Yanni must've noticed her white-knuckled grip on the arm-rest. 'It is not the traffic I am worrying about,' he confided. 'I have a good driver who is used to it and a comfortable coach. No, it is the weather.'

He looked out at the sky and shrugged. 'We will see. At this time of the year the rain is usually in the morning then the sunshine. Very good for the flowers,' he ended on an optimistic note.

To Stephanie the weather was also a worry. The imaginatively-named *Walk on the Wild Side* was a spring wildflower and gardens tour, and most of the time would be spent in the outdoors.

She shrugged, too. It was in the lap of the Gods. Hopefully, the tourists were all keen gardeners.

Like golfers, gardeners could be quite stoic when it came to uncomfortable conditions, their passion for the activity usually overcoming any hardships.

Stephanie wrapped her coat tightly about her as she stepped from the taxi into the cool morning. George, the hotel manager, came from his office to greet her and Yanni in the foyer.

'Ah, Miss Turner, it is good to see you again. I will have tea brought.' His welcoming smile deepened. 'You see, I remembered Greek coffee is too strong for you.'

Behind him, a long wall mirror reflected a dishevelled figure when Stephanie removed her coat. The combs that usually held back her shoulder-length dark hair had been knocked askew in the struggle to retrieve her case.

Automatically, her hand went to sweep away the escaping fine wisps.

It was a lost cause; a good brush and a fresh start was needed. But more seriously, a large, three-cornered tear in the back of her skirt flapped open to reveal bare legs as she moved.

It was hardly a good look for a tour leader, being more suited to a football player emerging from a rugby scrum.

Hastily, she donned her coat again to cover her discovery. 'Would you mind holding the tea for a little while?' she asked George. 'I'd like a couple of minutes in my room.'

Yanni had already settled himself at the table beside a potted palm. 'I will await you,' he announced, opening his briefcase.

The manager handed her key to the hovering porter. 'One of your party has already arrived, just before you.'

'Oh, yes, that will be William Brown, the wildflower expert from England,' Stephanie acknowledged.

The information was enough to send her hurrying toward the lift. Mr Brown shouldn't see her like this! It would be a bad start, especially if he was a dried-up academic of the old school who expected women to act like ladies at all times.

2

The next morning, cool and collected and glad her earlier arrival the day before had given her a chance to be that way, Stephanie watched as the hotel lobby filled with luggage and travellers.

They straggled in from the coach with Yanni, clothes crumpled, their faces tired and drawn in the artificial light. The long trip from Australia and pre-dawn arrival had taken its toll.

Stephanie counted her charges and checked their name-tags against her list, trying to impress on her memory the faces that went with each name. Fourteen. Good. Together with the as-yet-unseen wildflower expert, that made up the correct number of the group.

She supposed they wouldn't see William Brown before all met for lunch and took the scheduled wander through the Plaka. He'd remained out of sight since his arrival.

Looking around the weary faces, she decided to arrange with George for a later sitting of lunch if possible, to give them extra time to recover.

That meant the last member of the group would have to be advised of the change. She looked at her watch. It was far too early to ring his room; he wouldn't thank her for disturbing him at this hour. A note under his door would have to do.

'Breakfast, anyone? Or coffee? Come through to the dining-room while I fix up your keys and mark your luggage for delivery to your room.' She laughed at their reluctance to move away from Reception. 'I imagine your room is the only word that interests you. Fair enough.'

It was another hour before the book-work was completed and every-one settled. A mother and daughter, Harriet and Sue Pearson, expressed dissatisfaction with their front room and had to be relocated away from the street that was already waking to another working day.

Stephanie hoped they weren't going to prove difficult by demanding special attention.

Thankfully, she closed her bedroom door, kicked off her shoes and flopped on the bed. It had been an early morning start that needed all her concentration.

Too tired to take off her easy-care uniform, Stephanie stretched out and carefully pulled the light quilt over herself. She felt a glow of satisfaction. So far, things had gone smoothly; the coach arrived at the airport on time, despite the early hour, all her charges were well, no luggage had been mislaid.

Her body relaxed on the bed. A couple of hours rest before the amended lunch time —

The later lunch time! Stephanie was instantly alert. This was not the time to relax, everything had not been done!

How could she have forgotten the

wildflower expert, William Brown? If she didn't catch him before he went out, he could well be storming around in the dining-room at the advertised time, demanding his lunch.

Not that she expected to see him, even now. It was still an uncivilised hour; he was probably either asleep or, if an early riser, at least dressing. She decided the best idea was to slide a written message under his door without disturbing him.

She threw off the quilt, swung her legs to the side of the bed and fumbled with her feet for her shoes. Hastily scribbling a note giving the new arrangements, she put it in an envelope. A last-minute peek in the mirror assured Stephanie her appearance was unruffled by the moment of relaxation on the bed.

Most of the group, herself included, were accommodated on the same floor of the hotel. She phoned down to the receptionist and learned William Brown's room was on another floor.

Once out of the lift, it took only a matter of minutes to locate the room at the end of the corridor. Stephanie bent down to slip the envelope under the door.

Something was wrong — it didn't seem to be disappearing as it should. To her dismay, Stephanie realised the door was actually moving away from her. How had that happened? She hadn't knocked. Had the person inside heard her?

She straightened up, the envelope still in her hand. A polite smile on her lips.

'I'm Stephanie, the tour leader — ' she announced to the pyjama-clad figure that stood in the open doorway.

Even as she began to apologise, she wondered what twist of fate had brought the helpful stranger to this hotel of all the hotels in Athens. Had he followed her from the airport? She dismissed the idea as ridiculous, he had left the airport before her.

'I'm so sorry to disturb you,' she stammered.

'You haven't. I was expecting the maid with an extra towel I requested. What can I do for you?'

Stephanie could feel the red tide of embarrassment creeping up her neck. 'There's obviously a mistake in the room number I've been given.'

'It depends on whom you are looking for, doesn't it? Perhaps I can help you.'

The word 'again' hung unspoken on the air between them.

'Thank you, but I think not. I expected one of the members of my group to be in this room.' She backed away, adding a totally unnecessary explanation, not knowing why. 'He arrived early, a William Brown.'

The stranger reached out to claim the envelope with his left hand and extended his right to grip hers in greeting. With a smile that didn't quite reach his eyes, he said, 'I am he.'

3

Standing in the hotel corridor, shaking hands with a man in deep-blue pyjamas that mirrored his eyes, Stephanie was overcome by an Alice-in-Wonderland feeling. This was William Brown? This person about her own age?

She had been thinking of the wildflower expert as a bookish, older man, most probably a pipe-smoker in a cardigan.

How wrong she was! She hoped her astonishment didn't show. More than once she'd been told she had an expressive face. Was it giving her away again? The tips of her ears tingled with embarrassment.

As if on cue, a maid pushing a squeaking housekeeper's cart piled with towels, appeared at the other end of the corridor. Stephanie's blurred mind registered the sound of a vacuum cleaner starting up in a nearby room. At this time of the morning? It did seem a little unusual yet everything else was normal. Behind her the lift whirred upwards, a door banged.

William Brown obviously was not aware of the ridiculousness of the moment, making no attempt to hide his state of undress, quite at ease with the situation.

She became aware that William Brown, one eyebrow quirked, was waiting for her to speak.

'Why, welcome,' she said and, suddenly realising that her hand was still in his, abruptly dropped it.

Stephanie knew she should stay and deliver her message personally. It was the proper thing to do and he probably expected that, but all she wanted to do was escape.

'The note is self-explanatory. I'll see you at the new time.' The words came out in a rush.

She turned and, like a mouse confronted by a large cat, scuttled back to the safety of her room. Once inside, she leaned against the closed door, surprisingly breathless, all thoughts of resting gone, as she grappled with her embarrassment. What would he think of her as a tour leader? Would he be generous and see her as just another gauche Aussie?

It wasn't how she wanted to be seen. She prided herself on her efficiency.

What was done was done; she couldn't undo it. But she needed someone to restore her confidence.

She glanced at her watch and calculated the time difference between Greece and Australia. It would be close to midnight, but they kept late hours in her parents' house now that her father had taken early retirement and was no longer a slave to the alarm clock.

The sound of her mother's calm voice steadied her. 'Oh, Fanny, how lovely to hear from you. You've arrived safely, then.'

Stephanie smiled at the easy use of her pet name.

'Yes, Mum, everything is OK.'

And it was. There was no need to panic. She'd gotten off to a shaky start but she could handle it.

'Are you sure?'

'I thought I'd call you before I got busy. My group arrived safely, Yanni has all the details covered and I'm ready to go.'

'Don't do anything foolish, Fanny.' Her mother's voice deepened with concern. Stephanie wondered had Anne Turner read her daughter's mind. When she was young she'd been sure her mother was a gifted mind-reader, with supernatural powers. How else could she know what Stephanie was up to?

But, as she grew older, she learned that the feeling was the product of her own guilt, not her mother's psychic skills.

'Depends what you'd call foolish, Mum.' She deliberately made her answer light-hearted. 'Would doing a Shirley Valentine be called foolish?'

Her mother didn't laugh. 'Oh, Fanny, don't even think about it,' she admonished.

'Mum, you know your daughter is not likely to fall in love with a Greek waiter or a fisherman or do anything like that.'

'Does that mean you've given more thought to Martin's proposal? I saw him in the street yesterday, but I didn't know what to say.'

Stephanie really didn't want to think about Martin right now; all her energies were needed for the job on hand.

'He doesn't like the idea of you going overseas,' her mother went on.

No, it was more than that. Martin had always disliked her choice of a job, even when it was only flying around Australia. He wanted her to settle down, stay in one place, his and her birthplace, just like both their mothers had.

She changed the subject. 'How did Dad go in the bowls championship?'

'Your father can tell you all about it himself, Fanny. He's right here beside me.'

The details of her father's sporting

passion took quite a time. Stephanie found herself drawn into the life of the country town where everybody knew your name as Colin Turner mentioned his opponents, all remembered as fathers of friends from her childhood.

As she farewelled them both, she felt a wave of affection for her parents, and all they stood for, thankful for the good life they'd given her, their only child.

The hotel's small dining room was already buzzing with conversation between the rejuvenated travellers when William Brown made his appearance.

The chatter died immediately as the group eyed the newcomer to their midst.

The fair hair tamed, the pyjamas replaced by smart casual wear, he stood in the doorway like some golden Greek god in modern-day dress, his gaze sweeping the gathering until it settled on Stephanie.

For a split second she hesitated, unable to face him, reminded of their earlier meeting outside his room. What a fool she must've seemed, gawping at William Brown, holding his hand too long! Calling on all her professionalism, she got up from her seat and went to greet him.

'Ah, William, come and meet your ... er ... your companions ... your Australian companions on a *Walk On The Wild Side*.'

She turned and faced the dining room and, although the silence made it unnecessary, raised her voice to announce, 'Folks, may I introduce William Brown, our wildflower expert from England.'

There was a scraping of chairs on tiles as the men stood to shake hands, and room was made for him at the long table. It wasn't until everyone was settled that Stephanie realised an empty chair had been found between Sue and Harriet Pearson. Was it chance or had Sue, the youngest woman in the group, staked her claim?

Both mother and daughter offered William Brown choices from the array of delicacies being delivered to the table

27

with bewildering speed.

Traditional Greek salads appeared, together with little cheese pies, crispy fried courgette, aubergine, dolmades and a host of unfamiliar dishes.

From where she sat, half-way down the table, Stephanie could hear the Pearsons garnering as much information about William Brown as they could. Not quite quizzing him but close to it.

She found she was just as interested in the answers he gave to their questions, but the distractions of her duty to other members of the group meant she missed many of them.

As it happened, she learned very little about him, except that he lived in England, but exactly where was lost whilst she fielded an enquiry about the itinerary from the other lone, but less attractive, man on the tour, Ross Tremain.

'To allow people to fully recover from the flight, we're only going on a leisurely stroll around the Plaka this afternoon, not to the Acropolis. There will be a morning devoted to that on our return to Athens, but you may choose to go by yourself in your free time, Ross.'

She smiled at him, and, thinking his question had been answered, turned her head back to catch up with the Pearsons' cross-examination of William Brown.

'And what else do you do?' asked Harriet. 'Surely there can't be a living in this.' She waved her hand dismissively at the group.

There was a sharp intake of breath from the woman seated next to Stephanie, but William showed no sign of offence at the effrontery.

'I am usually successful at anything I undertake, Harriet,' he replied with good humour. 'In fact, if it is fair and honourable, I take pride in doing exactly what I want.'

The remarkable blue eyes swung away from the two women and encompassed the table.

Sue Pearson laughed flirtatiously. 'Oh, William, surely that must depend on what it is that you want. Does it apply to your personal life as well?'

Ross Tremain's belligerent voice cut across the provocative scene. 'An afternoon stroll around the Plaka is certainly not what I'd call a walk on the wild side,' he complained loudly. 'Why not continue on up to the Acropolis today? We'll be close by.'

Reluctantly, Stephanie gave him her full attention.

'I've already explained, Ross,' she said patiently, hoping he wasn't going to complain about every aspect of the tour. '*Walk on the Wild Side* is a play on words. I hope you understand that because there are no wildflowers in the city itself, things are a little more sedate.'

'Of course I do,' Ross protested. 'But not everyone wants to wander narrow old streets and look at shops,' he muttered. His face settled into a petulant droop more suited to a child than a grown man.

Stephanie tried to lighten his mood. 'Wait until we get to Crete, it'll be wild enough for you. This walk today is optional. It really is up to you, Ross. If you choose to come with us, departure time is at two fifteen in the foyer,' she answered, careful to keep her irritation under control. She consulted her watch. 'That's about twenty minutes. If you're not there, I'll know you've decided against coming. Right?'

Ross grunted, pushed his chair back and got up. It was the signal for others to leave the table, also, the Pearson women amongst them. Stephanie was surprised; she hadn't expected they would forsake their quarry so easily.

He didn't leave with the others, but merely moved farther up the table to pull out a chair opposite her and sit down.

'I've ordered tea for us,' he announced, leaning to one side to allow the waiter to clear the dishes from in front of him.

Stephanie hid her dismay. More tea!

Still, the caffeine might keep her alert. She was under no illusion that was what she needed to be to manage this diverse group of people.

'That was very thoughtful of you, William.'

'You're going to have trouble with Ross,' he commented, then laughed. 'I'd say we're in similar predicaments. Some people are amazingly persistent when it comes to being . . . difficult. Almost like . . . er . . . ferrets.'

It was a strange thing to say, but the image of the Pearson's blatant attempts to learn all about him was apt. She wished she could share the laugh but she intended to stick to the rules, and that meant no personal comments about members of the group. She stifled a titter.

'One of the things about our tours is we offer something different. This attracts all types of people,' she answered diplomatically and changed the subject to something more mundane. 'I'm so glad the weather is good.'

He took the hint and with a flicker of a smile, gravely discussed the weather.

William was right. In the days that followed, Ross Tremain proved very difficult. Stephanie found herself spending more and more time trying to bring him out of his brooding silence, without neglecting the other members of the group. There was an air about him that suggested a volcano about to erupt.

On the excursions they made to museums and archaeological sites she kept him supplied with information, but he showed little interest. Stephanie wondered how he came to be on this particular tour but hesitated to ask.

She was suffering a sense of failure about him when a retired army colonel and amateur historian, Bob McNeill, managed to elicit a response from him.

He talked to Ross of the strategies involved in the famous battle between the invading Persians and the Athenians, illustrating in the dust at their feet as they surveyed the Plain of Marathon.

Relieved to see her moody client

showing signs of animation at last, Stephanie walked away from the group gathered around the morning tea urn Yanni had set up beside the coach. The early fog had burned off to reveal a peaceful scent of vineyards and olive groves, thickly sprinkled with red wild poppies.

Nursing her tea, she stood apart, musing, enjoying a moment of quietude.

'It's hard to imagine this was the scene of such an important event that resulted in an Olympic Games race being named after it centuries later.'

William's voice startled her. It was the first time she'd actually been alone with him since the day of their encounter in the hotel corridor.

Now, suddenly, she was aware of her own position. She realised how much his diversionary tactics to save his own skin had taken the pressure off her, keeping the Pearsons from becoming a problem. Almost as if it had happened before. She was tempted to thank him.

Turning to look back at the coach and the group, she answered. 'Yes, there's a timelessness about Greece, and Yanni makes it all come alive, doesn't he? We're fortunate to have such a good guide, one with a way with people, backed up with a fund of knowledge of all things Greek, ancient and modern.'

'So you think he has a way with people, do you? Does he give you flowers?'

'Sorry?' She had to look at him now. He bent quickly to sweep up a bunch of poppies from the field.

'The colour of your lips,' he said, straight-faced, presenting them to her with an imperceptible bow.

Stephanie felt the heat rising from the v-neck of her shirt. 'And your cheeks,' he added. A teasing note had crept into his voice. 'But you haven't answered my question. Do you think Yanni is charming?'

'Of course I do. I would say everyone on the coach agrees with me. Our company has been fortunate to secure his services.'

She knew she was sounding more and more like a *Far Corners* Travel brochure.

'So it's not personal, then?'

Stephanie felt uneasy. Where was this going? More abruptly than she intended, she replied, 'No, it is not personal.'

'Ah, the lady doth protest too much, methinks.'

He was right, her response was out of proportion.

'Shakespeare seems out of place in ancient Greece, doesn't he?' She laughed lightly and began walking back toward the coach — and the approaching Pearsons.

William's muttered mild oath only made her laugh again, but genuinely this time.

'What is amusing you, Stephanie?' demanded Harriet Pearson suspiciously as they met.

'Would you believe, Shakespeare?'

'No,' said Sue, sourly, her eyes

darting between Stephanie and William.

Oh, lordy, another difficult client! Being a flight attendant had been easier than this. Stephanie suppressed the sigh and set about smoothing ruffled feathers.

Stephanie was late getting in to breakfast on the last day in Athens. She had been in George's office settling the account and using the telephone to confirm luncheon arrangements and the onward flight for later in the day.

A quick glance around the room located her group. She went from table to table reminding each one of day's travel arrangements.

'There's time for last minute shopping before we leave the city to catch the sun going down from the Temple of Poseidon at Cape Sunion. It's quite a sight. From there we make for the airport and our short flight to Crete.

'Has everyone put their suitcase outside their door for collection? Good. Remember, you'll need to keep your passport with you for security checks.

As we're travelling in a group we'll go through the check-in together.

'I have the tickets.'

Harriet put out an urgent hand to stop her as she passed. 'We have to speak to you, Stephanie.'

'What is it? Are either of you ill?'

'No, no, it's about William.'

Stephanie looked for William. He was chatting quite amicably with Marjory and Brian Gillespie at another table. Clearly something had happened to upset the Pearsons' established pattern of eating with him. Had the Gillespies usurped the Pearsons or had William himself taken a stand in desperation?

Whatever had happened this wasn't the time to worry about it. He was all right, that was clear and the possibility of losing her wildflower expert and exposing her total ignorance was eliminated.

Through the double doors Stephanie could see the porters emerging from the lifts with suitcases. She needed to check them. It would be disastrous if those belonging to her group became mixed with other departing coachloads.

'He seems all right, Harriet,' she answered distractedly.

The hand on her arm tightened.

'Ah, seems, that is the operative word —'

The foyer was filling with people and suitcases.

'I'm sorry, Harriet, but could you tell me about it later, please? Right now I'm needed out front.'

The Pearsons were not pleased, indignation written all over both faces.

'There's another, bigger group leaving and I'm worried about our luggage becoming mixed. Who knows where it could end up?' Her explanation made little difference to their expressions. 'I'm sorry,' she muttered and hurried away.

It was not a blue-sky day at Sunion. Low clouds hid all hope of a spectacular sunset and a cold wind whistling through the Doric columns drove all but the most ardent plant lovers indoors. Stephanie thought longingly of the warmth of the cafeteria as Yanni and William led them among the myriad species of wildflowers, until a short, sharp April shower made them race for cover.

Harriet Pearson was waiting for her just inside the door.

'I have something to tell you.'

The determined set of the woman's mouth told Stephanie she would have to postpone her planned cup of warming tea. She took Harriet's arm, and followed by Sue, led her to a quiet corner of the cafeteria.

'Now, what is it, Harriet?'

'William Brown is not who he says he is.'

4

Stephanie tried hard not to smile. She had expected Harriet's problem to be far more serious. Was this the result of William's efforts to shake off the matchmaking mother by having breakfast with the Gillespies?

She directed a meaningful glance toward the servery.

Harriet was not slow. 'Go and get Stephanie a cup of tea, Sue,' she ordered her daughter. 'Do you take milk, sugar, Stephanie?'

Stephanie shook her head in Sue's direction.

Harriet pulled her chair closer to the table and leaned forward to talk in a low, urgent voice. 'William claims to be a wildflower expert.'

'Yes, he has been employed by my company for that reason.'

The answer didn't seem to satisfy

Harriet. She said nothing, but her gimlet-like gaze didn't waver.

'We're lucky to have him,' Stephanie went on. 'I know nothing whatsoever about plants, and Yanni is here to look after the local issues. We couldn't do without him either.'

'He says he's from Kew Gardens in London,' Harriet said, pausing to wait for Stephanie's reaction.

'Harriet, this really isn't anything to do with me. As I said, *Far Corners* engaged him. I just work for them. Although I must say it isn't really work, being in Greece.' And, hoping to defuse the woman's dissatisfaction, added with a smile, 'Nor is looking after you all.'

Harriet didn't seem impressed by the diplomatic explanation. She dismissed it with a wave of her hand.

'But you don't understand,' she insisted. 'We've been on to the internet and can't find any trace of him there — '

'Harriet, this isn't anything to do with me,' Stephanie repeated.

'Isn't it?' Harriet demanded. 'You seem to get along fine with him.'

It was ridiculous. As calmly as she could, Stephanie answered. 'I hope I get along fine with all of you. As I said, the arrangements the company make are not for me to question. I am here to do the best I can to make sure your tour runs smoothly. In regard to William, my only concern is that he shares his knowledge with you — ' She smiled at the angry woman. 'And has a valid passport.'

Harriet's manner became even more intense. 'Ah. yes, a passport! That's where you come in.'

Sue arrived back with a cup of tea. Stephanie seized on it almost eagerly, wrapping both her still-cold hands around the cup. She hoped drinking it would give her breathing space, time to choose her words carefully.

But Harriet only allowed her one sip before she revealed what they had in mind for her.

'You could ask to see his passport — '

'What?' Stephanie spluttered in surprise, putting down her cup with a clatter.

'We don't think he's given his real name, you see. I mean, William Brown!' Sue was scornful.

Stephanie took up her cup again and gazed at the two women over its rim, trying to gauge the seriousness of their suggestion. There was no doubt they expected her to comply.

Stephanie hadn't seen any written company policy forbidding her to enquire into another employee's private life, but she thought it was as good an excuse as any to hide away.

'I'm sorry, but that is out of the question. For one thing, there is no reason I could give for such a request, but more importantly, it would be against company policy to pry into a client's private life.'

Harriet was quick to catch her out. 'He's not a client!' she said. 'He's one of your own. Are you trying to cover something up?'

Stephanie sighed. Whatever she said she couldn't win. 'Harriet, I'd rather you asked him yourself if you feel so strongly. I hope you understand, I can't do it — we have to work together,' she added, trying to soften the refusal with a smile.

The Pearson women were not in a mood to accept her apology; they sat stony-faced and silent. Stephanie wondered should she offer to pay for the cup of tea. She was scrabbling in her satchel for her purse when Yanni joined them.

'Is it time to round up the troops, Yanni?' she enquired brightly, passing the euros across the table to Sue. 'Thanks for getting me the tea,' she smiled and got up. 'If you'll both excuse me while I go count heads . . .'

The Pearsons' outrageous request was very much on Stephanie's mind as she assembled the group and outlined details of the trip cross-country to the airport. 'It's a group check-in, so after that, just make your way individually

45

through security and Customs. With your passport, of course.'

She felt the weight of the Pearsons' expectations again at the airport when passports had to be produced to proceed through security and yet again to board the buses that ferried them to their aircraft.

She knew the two women were watching for an opportunity in the departure lounge, ready to learn what they could about William, with or without her help. Harriet didn't look like a woman who gave up easily, but then, he was a grown man and hardly needed looking after. All Stephanie could hope for was that their displeasure wouldn't affect the others.

The flight to Crete was short, and it was not yet dark when they arrived at the hotel on the waterfront in Chania. To her surprise, Eleni, the owner, asked for passports. 'Government regulations. I shall return them tomorrow,' she said.

Passports? Stephanie laughed to herself at the coincidence as she went around the group waiting in the lounge, gathering their passports. Harriet Pearson gave her a meaningful nod when there was one person missing.

Stephanie turned, looking for him. 'Hey, William! No passport, no key.'

'Later,' he called, disappearing into the bar with Yanni.

The porters were chalking the luggage with room numbers, and loading the bags into the lift.

'Dinner is in the taverna next door. We have time for a freshen-up,' she said as she handed out the keys.

It was not until Stephanie was lying in bed later that night that the idea of checking William's identity began to niggle. She shifted her mind off what the Pearsons had asked of her to their reason for asking.

William was not whom he claimed to be? Leaving aside the fact it was none of their business, should she make it her business? Did her responsibility to the *Far Corners Travel Company* extend that far? He had been hired for his specialist knowledge and seemed to be doing a good job sharing that.

The Pearsons, by their ruthless pursuit of William, had put a doubt in her mind. Earlier in the evening, he had brushed off her request for his passport. Did what she saw as merely a ruse to avoid the determined women have an ulterior motive?

5

It was a free day. After breakfast, Stephanie began to explore the old town around the Venetian harbour, alone, and glad to be away from responsibility.

She criss-crossed the steep back streets, delighting in the twisting thoroughfares, the nooks and crannies — and the cats. Sleek and well-tolerated, they draped themselves over steps and low walls, deigning to be petted or played with by children and passers-by.

Only a few tourists penetrated this far; most preferred the waterfront. Craggy-faced Cretans, gathered in dark, men-only cafés, called a greeting as she passed, and the housewives bustling about their marketing in their traditional black, were all smiles for her.

It was so typically Greek, Stephanie

wasn't expecting the fair-haired girl who rounded a corner and cannoned into her with a shower of documents and a string of foreign words that was either a curse or an apology.

She took a quick look at Stephanie as she bent to retrieve her papers from the cobbled lane-way before the wind carried them out of reach. 'Oops, I'm sorry. I didn't realise you were English.'

Stephanie joined in the chase. 'I'm not,' she called over her shoulder.

'Did I hurt you? I really will have to slow down. If you're not English, where are you from?' The questions were delivered rapid-fire in a Scottish accent as the girl bobbed up and down.

'Australia,' Stephanie answered, bending to help with the recovery of the last of the papers.

'Thanks. I'm Fiona Campbell.' She tidied the bundle, tucked it under one arm and put out her free hand. 'I'm in the travel business — '

'Why, so am I! I'm a tour leader.'

'You are? Had any falls?'

'Any falls?'

Fiona laughed. 'It's how tour leaders greet each other. The possibility of one of their clients falling and injuring themselves is a continuing nightmare. You must be new not to have heard it.'

'I am. Very new.'

'What people get up to on holidays doesn't bear thinking about. They seem to leave their commonsense at home and take terrible risks.' She paused for a moment and glanced at her watch.

'Look, I'm really on business, checking out an eating place that I can recommend to my people as a genuine Cretan experience. Is it too early for your lunch? I could do with another opinion, especially one from an Australian.'

She hardly waited for an answer and led Stephanie into a nearby taverna. The owner came forward with a menu and found them a table overlooking a miniscule walled garden shaded by an old bay tree.

'New management, country cooking,'

Fiona murmured behind the menu. The serious business of ordering out of the way, she became quite animated again. 'Now, tell me something about yourself. Where do you go from here?'

Stephanie outlined the itinerary. 'As I said, this is my first trip. I'm on short-term contract, trip by trip. It's not very satisfactory, but I was glad to get the job. Hundreds of us were thrown out of work by an airline collapse. Of course, now I'm here I'm over the moon.'

'What will you do if the contract isn't renewed?'

'Don't even talk about that possibility!'

Fiona laughed and turned to attract the attention to the waiter.

'That's a mark against the place,' she confided a little scornfully. 'He's now hovering because he can tell I'm not interested in a summer love.'

'A summer love?'

'That's the name given to flings the locals have with the holiday-makers.' The waiter had returned her card.

'Let's get out of here.'

They stepped out into the brilliant sunshine. 'My office is just around the corner,' Fiona said, leading the way up the narrow street.

'Tell me more about summer loves,' Stephanie prompted. 'Does it go on very much?'

Fiona laughed. 'It's part of the package deal, holiday, sun, handsome Greek men, it's irresistible. Girls think they are in love, but of course, it is only for the summer. They return home, don't hear from their young man, and, after a little while, they forget. The waiters and the fishermen know all along how it will end.' She shrugged. 'Winter comes. That's why they call it a summer love.'

'Not life-changing like Shirley Valentine, then?'

'Well, a little bit. Depends on how soon you can get over a broken heart, I suppose.'

Laughing at the foolishness of women, Stephanie allowed Fiona to lead her through a maze of back streets. It was in one of them that they came upon a taverna that was no more than a hole in the wall. A bright, fair head stood out in its darkness.

Without knowing why, Stephanie shrank back against the stone wall. Harriet's questions about William's true identity returned. What was William doing in such an out-of-the-way part of town? She had taken it for granted that, like her, he was a newcomer to Greece. But he obviously knew his way around. And who was his dark companion? The conversation between them seemed earnest.

'What is it?' Fiona asked.

Something warned Stephanie William might not welcome being seen. 'Is there another way?'

Fiona's gaze went from her to the figure of William. Without a word, she turned and steered Stephanie down another alleyway.

'Almost there,' the Scottish girl encouraged her up a particularly steep incline. And, as if she knew Stephanie would be wondering, she pointed out a wide street ahead. 'That'll take you to the harbour-front.'

'Why aren't you down there where the tourists are?'

'My business is not off-the-street. I do wholesale, dealing with companies like yours.' She inserted a key in the door of a nondescript office and flung it wide, dumping her bundle of documents on the floor.

'Now, tell me who that interesting man was. And why you didn't want to introduce us. Is he your summer love?'

Out of breath from the steep climb, Stephanie quickly denied it. She was tempted to confide in this likeable, new-found friend, but decided against it. The Pearsons were being rather silly, anyway.

'No, no, not mine, but I think someone in my group would like him to be more than that,' she replied.

Stephanie liked to make herself available to her clients for an hour at the end of free days, just in case they had encountered any difficulties on their own.

She sat in the hotel lounge overlooking the sea-wall and the marina with its yachts bobbing gently in the swell, halyards slapping hollowly against aluminium masts.

Eleni came from behind the reception desk and handed Stephanie her passport.

'Thank you, Eleni, I had forgotten about it.' And that was true. She'd managed to enjoy the day without thinking too much about passports and true identities and the demands of the Pearson women.

'We have the same birthday, you and I, but I have had it longer than you.' Eleni laughed and put up a hand to the crows' feet around her eyes.

As she spoke, the glass doors swung open to admit Yanni and William. Their faces reddened by exposure to the sun and wind, they brought with them the smell of the sea.

'Have you collected your passport, William?' Stephanie asked. He nodded. 'Would you believe Eleni and I share a birthday?'

'Don't say the obvious, William. I already have,' Eleni joked as she walked back to her desk.

Stephanie stared after her. William? That was rather familiar, wasn't it? He was only a guest in her hotel, after all. Was this the famous Greek hospitality or something more?

The two men flopped into the comfortable chairs and William ordered drinks for the three of them.

'We've been sailing. And what did you do today, Stephanie?' he asked, fishing in his pocket for coins to pay the waiter.

Despite her intention to ignore Harriet's claim, Stephanie thought that was strange. Why wasn't he using plastic? Or charging the drinks to his hotel account? Was it because he would have to sign his name? His real name?

'Stephanie!'

'Sorry, what was that?'

'Your day?'

'Oh, I met a Scottish girl in the travel business and we had lunch together.'

Yanni leaned toward her. 'Would that be Fiona Campbell?'

Stephanie nodded, not surprised by his question; there probably was only a small community that served the large number of tourists, and they would know each other.

'What did she want?' he asked suspiciously.

'Why, just my opinion on a taverna under new management.'

Yanni and William exchanged looks. 'Where was that?' It was William who was quizzing her now. Was it just her imagination that there was anxious tone to his voice?

'Did Fiona ask any special questions?' asked Yanni without waiting for her to answer William.

'Not unless you think, did I like the food, a special question. Hey, guys, what's with you two?'

'Nothing,' they both replied at once.

'Yanni is afraid you may've given away trade secrets. It's cut-throat, the tour business.'

Secrets? Were secrets being discussed in a hidden taverna in a back street? Stephanie gave him a long, hard look, but there was nothing to be learned from the handsome face. In any case, it wasn't anything to do with her. He could have as many clandestine meetings as he wished.

'She also asked me if I'd had any falls. I'd never heard that before and thought she meant me personally.'

They were still laughing when a crowd, dressed for dinner, spilled from the lift. It included Harriet and Sue. Stephanie sighed. From the look on Harriet's face, it wasn't hard to guess what the woman was thinking. And expecting.

The group moved out of the hotel, the women in high heels picking their way carefully across the cobbled promenade to a nearby taverna. Bouzouki music poured into the night from the upstairs windows. Stephanie felt her excitement rising.

Impulsively, she turned to the person nearest her. It was William.

'It doesn't get any better than this,' she confided.

The light from the doorway caught William's hair but his face was in the shadows.

'You're enjoying this tour, aren't you?'

'Yes,' she answered simply. 'It's not the first time I've been to Greece, I was here six months ago. But there's something about . . . ' She looked up at him. 'This time,' she trailed off.

'Come along everyone,' Yanni called from the top of the stairs. The group moved forward and William's arm was at her back, shepherding her up into a room already filling with tourists.

For Stephanie, the evening passed in a dream, the food, retsina, the laughter, the music, one magical blur. It became later and later, but no-one looked to return to the hotel. Even Ross Tremain's usually sullen face relaxed.

The coffee was being served when the taverna owner signalled the music-makers, and encouraged Yanni to his feet. With their arms on each other's shoulders, the two men began to dance.

The music changed, the taverna owner went back to his kitchen, and Yanni, still in a dancing mood, coaxed Stephanie out of her chair.

Protesting her ignorance of the steps, she let him take her hand and lead her to dance side by side with him, her arm bent at the elbows, hands held high, as she copied his basic slow-quick-slow movements. Encouraged by her example, others got up and formed a line that moved counter-clockwise around the floor, gathering diners as it passed their table.

Stephanie felt William's grip on her wrist as he loosened Yanni's hold and then the warmth of his hand in hers.

The music changed again, became wilder, the line broke up as the inexperienced tourists dropped out. The man on her other side let go. With a flourish, William twirled her around to face him, in a decidedly un-Greek way, leaving Yanni to dance on his own.

Breathless, she let herself soften in William's arms and, with the sheer pleasure of the moment, laughed up into his face. For a brief moment, their eyes met, their bodies touched.

His embrace tightened, then let go.

6

The knocking woke Stephanie. She sat up with a start, her heart beating wildly, and focused her eyes on the digital clock-face glowing in the dark. Who would be at her door at two o'clock in the morning? Certainly not one of the members of her group needing help — to protect her privacy, her room number was not divulged to them. Any crisis call would come through the hotel reception desk.

It wouldn't be Yanni, either. He would have telephoned first, such was his respectful manner toward her.

That left William — and her behaviour. Perhaps she'd been foolish, even indiscreet, letting herself be carried away by the magic of the night and the music. Although at the end of the dance there had been a circle approving smiles it had not included the Pearsons.

The knocking came again, soft but insistent.

She could ignore it no longer. If it was William, he obviously was not going to stop until she sent him away, her fumbling hand found the bedside lamp and switched it on.

With one decisive movement she threw back the bedclothes and got up. The room was not large and she was tying her robe when she reached the door and unlatched the chain.

The dimly-lit corridor was empty.

Stephanie stood for a moment in the open doorway, puzzled. Had her nocturnal visitor tired of waiting for her response? Surely not; she'd moved quickly after she'd heard the second summons. She had to ask herself if she'd only dreamed someone was knocking. That was a possibility, but no, the sound continued after she woke.

And was continuing now!

With a smile at her foolishness, and glad no-one was there to witness it, Stephanie quietly closed the door. She crossed the room, parted the billowing scrims and pulled shut the glass door that led on to the balcony.

With it no longer swinging in the rising wind and banging against an outdoor chair, the noise ceased. Only the muted sounds of the harbour reached her.

It was the day for the long walk from one of Crete's highest villages with its spectacular views down through a deep gorge to the sea at Komitades. Because of the ruggedness of the terrain only the really dedicated walkers were going. They gathered around Yanni, leaving the smaller number of non-walkers with Stephanie.

To her dismay, her charges included William. Her heart sank. In the bustle of the morning departure, it had been easy enough to avoid facing him.

Yanni and his band of hikers climbed out of the village and soon became tiny figures dwarfed by the towering land-scape, then disappeared.

Stephanie called her group together.

Apart from William, the Pearsons and the elderly Gillespies, she faced the day in the company of the sullen Ross, who was a non-action man as well as a malcontent.

She also had a problem with Marion, a divorcee who took no part in any walking, often sitting in the coach reading a book. She wouldn't come to life until nightfall.

'We're going to take the coach to meet Yanni and the hikers at Komitades,' she explained. 'This doesn't mean we won't be seeing any wildflowers. There will be a short walk into the gorge from the other end. And we're lucky to have William with us to tell us all about them.

'There will be time to wander on the beach before lunch in the taverna there. The weather has been kind to us today. It should be a very pleasant time in a very pleasant place.'

And it was; even the bored Marion was enticed out of the coach to wander the beach. The taverna snuggled into the sandhills almost at the water's edge, open to the breezes on two sides.

Looking out to sea there was no visible line between the blue water and the same blue of the sky. The surf was beating rhythmically on the shoreline, leaving a residue of froth on the sand.

The handsome owner of the taverna spoke excellent English and was called Stefanos. Delighted by the similarity of their names, he took Stephanie into the kitchen and introduced her to his wife and daughter.

They wandered back into the eating area. 'You have a wonderful position here,' remarked Stephanie.

Stefanos nodded proudly. 'My father started with just a shack before I was born. Now I carry on every summer and my son, Nicholas, he will take over after me. He is a good boy, working with his grandfather on the farm where we grow everything we serve, even the wine. You will have some?'

'No, Stefanos, she'd prefer a cup of tea, I know her,' said William.

Stephanie swung round at the sound of his voice. When she last looked, he had been on the beach with the Gillespies. He had left the elderly, slow-moving couple behind, probably at their urging, and come to stand, tall and fair, beside the dark Cretan. A complete contrast.

'As a matter of fact, I would. Save the wine for later, with the meal, thank you, Stefanos.'

She looked around the taverna, chose a table and sat down. William joined her.

'This is an ideal spot, isn't it? I'm able to sit here and enjoy my tea with my eye on my charges,' she said, waving an arm in their direction and hoping some of them would come soon. Even the Pearsons would be welcome!

'What are we going to do about us?'

Startled, Stephanie turned her head sharply toward William.

'What did you say?' she asked, quite forgetting her vow not to become personal with him. Or with anyone. A squadron of jets from a nearby air-base screamed overhead and drowned his answer.

At that moment, Stefanos brought the tea, then excused himself to lower the clear plastic blinds on the windward side of the taverna.

'The guests might not like too much sea-breeze while they eat,' he explained before returning to the kitchen to supervise the preparation of the meal.

After the interruption, Stephanie returned her gaze to William, expecting him to answer her question. Instead, he casually asked another, seemingly unconnected one.

'Where would we be without plastic?'

'If the wind got up? Sheltering in the coach, I imagine.' Telling herself she'd misheard his previous remark, Stephanie gave a little laugh and followed his gaze to the entrance to the taverna. The hikers and non-hikers had met and were converging on the rest-rooms.

She and William were no longer alone. Only Marion remained at the far end of the beach, surrounded by a pack of dogs. With horrified fascination, Stephanie watched as the woman handed out food to the strays. Hadn't she heard of rabies? Uneasy, she picked up Tom Gillespie's walking stick from behind his chair with a brief 'May I?' and stepped out on to the sand. But she was already too late.

Some of the dogs had begun to fight over the scraps, snarling and showing their teeth. Others were leaping to tear the food from Marion's hands. Frightened, she was backing away, screaming and futilely waving her hands in the air.

Stephanie began to run. At first, the threat of someone with a stick had little effect on the scavenging dogs; they were at their most primitive. Petrified, the woman stood in their midst, buffeted as they leapt higher and higher for a bag clutched tightly in one of her hands.

'Drop the food, Marion!' she ordered over and over.

It was useless; the screaming had become so hysterical she doubted Marion even heard. Stephanie looked over her shoulder. Help was coming but not soon enough.

She moved closer to the melee, wielding the walking stick more vigorously to keep the dogs from mistaking her legs for something else to be fought over. Snatching the bag of food from the woman, she tossed it away. The dogs followed, intensifying their fighting, ripping the bag to pieces between them in a frenzy of disputed possession.

William and Yanni were the first to reach the scene.

'Come on, Marion, it's all over,' Yanni consoled the distraught woman. He gently persuaded her back down the beach toward the taverna and the rest of the open-mouthed group.

Wordlessly, William reached out to embrace Stephanie, then, as if thinking better of it, dropped his arms. For a long moment, he blocked her way, his eyes keenly searching her face before nodding and letting her pass. Side by side, they continued the short distance over the sand to join the group.

'That was quite a fight you put up, Steph. Well done!'

Stephanie wasn't sure who had said that, but knew it certainly wasn't William. He had disappeared.

Marion was calmed and checked for bites. Stefanos brought glasses and a bottle of ouzo from the bar, and encouraged her to drink. Satisfied there was no harm done, Marjorie Gillespie took the still-shaking woman to the washroom.

Stephanie felt gentle hands on her shoulder propelling her to a chair. Suddenly weak-kneed, she sank down and gulped the fiery drink William pressed on her. It steadied her.

'I'm sorry I didn't notice what was happening soon enough,' he murmured, the face close to hers intent with regret. 'You could've been bitten.'

Her shakiness increased at the thought and the concern in his voice. She realised it would be so easy to break down and slip into sympathetic arms.

'No worries! I knew I'd had my

shots,' she said with a flash of bravado to cover her desire to be cosseted until her heartbeat returned to normal.

Tom Gillespie came to reclaim his walking stick. 'Thank you, Tom, it did a super job,' she said, handing it back.

'And so did you, young lady. I wouldn't like to get in the way when you mean business.'

Suddenly she was surrounded, the centre of attention, and William was being pushed into the background.

'Now that's what I call taking your job seriously,' boomed the Colonel, ruddy-faced from the morning's hike. 'Darned dangerous.'

'Whatever happened?' asked Harriet, coming from the toilets and obviously bewildered by all the fuss.

For once, Sue had seen more than her mother. 'Marion was feeding the dogs again and they turned on her.'

'What do you mean, Sue?' asked Stephanie. 'Has she done it before?'

'Yes, every day. If there isn't any meat to take from the breakfast buffet, she buys packets of biscuits to feed the stray dogs everywhere we go.'

Stephanie bit back her annoyance at such foolishness. Her new friend, Fiona, had been right. Some people do leave their commonsense at home when they go on holidays.

The ouzo had done its work. Restored, she stood up and resumed her duties.

'Come along, everyone! Stefanos and his family have prepared a wonderful home-grown lunch especially for us. Let's enjoy it!'

At day's end, Stephanie longed for some stillness after the demands made by the eventful outing. As if the incident with the dogs hadn't been stressful enough, she felt obliged to talk with Marion in her room about the dangers of her behaviour. It was a waste of time — Marion was unrepentant.

'They were starving!' she protested self-righteously.

'All the more reason to leave them be, I would think, Marion.'

'I can't do that, I'm an animal lover.'

'They were feral, Marion, not domesticated animals like you see on the streets at home. You put yourself in great danger.'

'I don't care about that!'

Stephanie decided to get tough. 'Well, I'm sorry, but I do. You put other members of the group at risk and, as leader, I must ask you to stop the practice.'

Marion's mutinous face told her this was not the way to win friends. Stephanie shrugged her shoulders at the stubbornness of the woman and, barely containing her anger, left the room.

From the foyer she could see the sea-wall was deserted. Snatching at the opportunity to be alone, she hurried out of the hotel, past the historic old shipyards and up the stone steps.

In marked contrast to the sheltered harbour, the open sea pounded on the breakwater rocks, as it had done for centuries. There was something about its action that reflected her emotions, her frustration crashing up against the need to remain calm. Staying that way was important if she was to succeed in her new job.

It was hard; the memory of the frightening pack of wild dogs as she saved Marion from her foolishness was still fresh.

Determined to put it behind her, her mind went on to remember the most enjoyable aspects of the day. The taverna on the beach, Stefanos, the lunch, everyone's concern. And William's solicitude.

Was it far-fetched to think he'd tried to get her alone before the incident of the dogs? Had he intended to take her up on what could've been misinterpreted as an invitation when they danced the night before? He'd left the Gillespies behind but that could've been because he wasn't a beach person. And nothing to do with her.

She also questioned if she'd misheard him and, because she was feeling embarrassed about her behaviour, thought he'd asked her a personal question. Had he only asked what are we going to do, meaning the members of the group, and her plans for the rest of the outing?

That made sense. A man as attractive as he would have so many women responding to him, from the most blatant, like Sue Pearson, to the merest flicker of interest. He would come to expect it. Was it too much to hope he hadn't misread her actions at all, perhaps hadn't even noticed?

Just as she had to cope with Marion, her job required her to keep her distance from romantic entanglement, real or imagined, on the client's part or on her own.

She looked back across the harbour to the hotel. The last rays of the sun were glinting on its windows. Behind them, the group, with its undercurrents, would be assembling in the bar for pre-dinner drinks.

Could she manage to juggle the different demands being made on her?

7

The deep, narrow valley, its slopes covered by wild daphne bushes, was hidden high in the stark mountains. Costas parked the coach under an ancient tree at the entrance and produced a folding table and a number of camping stools. Working quickly, Yanni and Stephanie opened the picnic lunch.

Later, the climb into the valley began easily enough, with Yanni leading the way. At home in the mountains, he exchanged boisterous greetings with the shepherds working on sheep near their basic stone hut.

As they climbed higher, Yanni warned everyone to stay on the track in single file until, he promised, it opened out into flat areas.

'Plenty of wildflowers there,' he called over his shoulder. 'But, for now, just follow me, please. There are loose rocks that make the mountainside very dangerous.'

In the rear of the group, Stephanie was having trouble with Ross Tremain. He was scouting round looking for a break in the roadside rock-face.

'This road is not very good for photographs,' he complained. 'Needs more height. I reckon I could do better from up there.' He had already found a foothold.

'Yanni says it's basically unstable, Ross,' Stephanie remonstrated to his back. He kept going.

'Wait!' she called in a more urgent voice, but the figure in the red, all-weather coat and leather hat had already disappeared among the boulders. She wondered was it a gender issue. Would he take more notice of a man? Should she appeal to Yanni?

'Stephanie!'

She hurried forward to answer a call from the tail-end of the party.

'There's an old man up front and he

doesn't seem very pleased.'

She caught up with Yanni. He was being confronted by an old shepherd with a can strapped to his back.

'What is he saying?' she asked.

'He says us being in the hills is disturbing his sheep and goats. It will spoil their milk. That is what he has in the can on his back. He is taking it down to the village.'

Stephanie looked around her. 'What village?'

Yanni spoke again and the old man pointed down into the chasm. She could see nothing that resembled a village, only rocks.

'Will he walk down there?' she asked in astonishment.

There was a further exchange of questions and answers in Greek before the shepherd's manner changed. A wide smile revealed a mouth of gappy, yellow teeth.

'It is all right — you are Australians,' Yanni translated. 'He remembers when he was a boy, the Germans invaded his island during the Second World War, trapping many Australian soldiers. His father and neighbours sheltered them in their houses and in caves up here in the mountains and eventually helped them escape to Cairo by boat.'

'Tell him we're proud to shake his hand,' said Stephanie, looking around the gathered group for their agreement.

'Cairo,' repeated the old man as he shook each hand. Adjusting his milk-can, he trudged off down a goat-track that clung to the side of the mountain.

Before long, as Yanni had promised, the climb plateaued out into high meadows of wildflowers. William moved among the delighted group, naming the different varieties.

Afternoon shadows began to creep across the valley below, and with them, the suggestion of a chilly night ahead.

'Come on, everyone, it's time to return to Chania,' called Stephanie, turning back down the mountain toward the waiting coach.

'I got a good shot of the old fellow,'

announced Bob McNeill as he settled in his seat and packed away his camera. 'I'm going to write an article for a veterans' magazine back in Australia. There's bound to be some interest.'

Stephanie began her head-count.

It was one short. She checked again — still one short. Slowly, she walked down the aisle, stopping at each seat until she found one that was vacant. 'Who's missing? Who was sitting here on the way out?'

'Ross was.'

Of course. How could she have missed him? She fought back her annoyance. Distracted by the arrival of the old shepherd, she'd forgotten about Ross setting off to climb higher for a better photo of the valley and the mountains beyond. What was keeping him? It was still light, but conditions suitable for panoramic pictures certainly couldn't last much longer.

'Yanni, we'll have to go back and

hurry him up,' she said, then added a reassuring word to the rest of the group. 'We won't be long, folks.'

'I blame myself for not keeping an eye on him,' Stephanie confided to Yanni as they hurried up the track past the shepherds' hut. The sheep and goats had been herded into their night enclosures, but there was no sign of the shepherds or the old man.

'He will be in his village by now,' said Yanni.

'What a wonderfully fit man for his age,' she commented as the climb began. Soon, walking over the rough ground began to pull at the muscles in the back of her legs. Up this testing track twice in one day was more than she'd expected when they set off that morning.

The light was quite bad by the time they reached the spot where Stephanie thought she'd last seen Ross. Carefully, they began to climb among the rocks, calling as they went, pausing at intervals to listen for a reply. Not even the sound of thunking goat-bells disturbed the silence.

The air was crisp and crystal clear and already a hint of overnight frost lay on the ground. She shivered.

Behind them, a voice called. Hopefully, they both turned to answer.

'Ross?'

'No, it's William.'

He was right beside them, scarcely out of breath. That would come from working outdoors, Stephanie decided, then remembered the softness of the hand clasping hers during the dancing in the tavern. It certainly wasn't the hand of a manual worker.

'You've been gone a while. I decided you may've encountered trouble and could probably do with an extra pair of eyes. Three of us should make short work of the search.'

'Are the group becoming restless?' she asked anxiously.

'No, everyone understands. Costas is running the heating so they're comfortable. I borrowed his flashlight and brought an extra bottle of water and some oranges.'

'Thank you for coming, William. It's getting dark and the sooner we find Ross, the better.'

As they spread out, her heart quailed at the prospect of what they were looking for. However positively she tried to sound, there couldn't be a good outcome now.

She switched on her torch and swung the beam into a dark crevice underlying a huge rock that jutted out over the path above them and called again.

A low answering groan beyond the circle of light was the first indication that Ross had been found. As her flashlight swept the area, it revealed a red-coated huddle.

Even as relief swept over her, Stephanie felt a rush of self-pity. Of all the things to happen on her first trip! She scrambled over the rocks and knelt beside Ross, lifting his head to gently dribble bottled water on to his dry lips.

'I fell,' Ross informed her unnecessarily, his voice barely a whisper. No wonder they hadn't heard his response to their calls until she was right upon him.

'Crawled in here . . . out of the cold.'

Stephanie supposed she was expecting too much, that he would express his regret at the trouble he was causing — the man was obviously in great pain. She ran her hands over his limbs, her heart sinking as she felt the twist in his right leg.

Satisfying herself the lacerations to his face and hands were only superficial, she turned her head to call Yanni and William. They came and knelt beside her, their faces grave in the glow of their flashlights.

'We can't move him without splints of some sort.' Despair coloured her voice. 'There's no hope of getting him down from here without help, is there, Yanni?'

Yanni was already trying his mobile. 'I am afraid we are out of range,' he reported, pocketing it.

'Would it be any better down at a lower level?'

'I could try, but I'm not sure.'

Stephanie's mind was in emergency mode. 'The best thing for you to do would be to return to the coach, and if it doesn't work there, drive on to the village and summon help. Oh, and ask Costas to take the clients back to the hotel.'

'But what about you? I cannot leave you here,' Yanni protested.

'Excuse me, may I make a suggestion?' William broke in. 'I will stay here with Stephanie.'

William's offer sent Stephanie into a spin. She wondered what the Tour Leader's Manual would say about allowing a client to spend a cold night on a mountain. But was he a client? Wasn't he a company employee, too? She certainly didn't like the idea of being alone in the dark waiting for help to arrive.

Yanni obviously liked the plan. Even

as she voiced her objections, he said, 'I would be happier if William stayed with you, Stephanie. It will be a long wait.'

'It's settled, then,' said William, taking off his coat and covering Ross's lower body and twisted leg. 'I'll go down as far as the shepherds' hut with you, Yanni, and see if I can find something warm. I noticed drifts of late snow on the higher reaches earlier today. The temperature is dropping already, and it could get quite cold before long. Sorry, Stephanie, but I'll be as quick as I can.'

'It's all right, William,' Stephanie answered, trying to sound more confident than she felt. She wondered what wild animals roamed the hills; the sheep and goats weren't yarded every night without a reason.

She watched the two men set off, their dark silhouettes against the evening sky a comfort to her until they reached the lower track and disappeared.

She'd agreed to the arrangements as being the only sensible way but she hadn't expected to feel so alone. All her hypothetical emergency training as a flight attendant hadn't prepared her for the burden of an injured man on a remote mountainside in Crete.

8

She settled herself in the narrow crevice beside Ross and took one of his hands in hers. He stirred, returned her grip but made no attempt to speak.

There was no sense of time. A weak moon rose in the sky, faintly outlining the boulders. It would make walking a little easier for Yanni and William, and eventually, the rescuers. Even so, it was still dark.

A bleak thought crossed her mind — what if William couldn't find her again? He wouldn't have the mountain skills of a local, and wouldn't recognise any distinguishing landmarks. There was no way she could waste her batteries by leaving her flashlight on indefinitely to guide him.

She wondered how the group were coping. If she was any judge of character, Bob McNeill would have taken over, ensured they were delivered safely and escorted them to dinner in the taverna next to the hotel.

Thinking of dinner, she wished she was in the warmth of the taverna right now, with a good slug of ouzo to get the circulation going.

Stephanie had no idea how long she'd been sitting in the dark when a noise disturbed her. She straightened up with a start and stared into the night. Rocks were skittering down the slope below but there was no reassuring glow of a flashlight.

Was it a wild animal? Or a sheep or goat that had missed the shepherds' nightly round-up? That was hardly likely with such small flocks. They probably all had names and one would be missed immediately.

Her mouth twisted at the irony; she, too, had a small flock and knew their names, yet had managed to lose one of them.

The crunching sounds were getting nearer. Stephanie crouched lower over

Ross's body, her pulse racing. Could she hope that whatever it was would change direction before it reached them? Should she lie quietly or make a noise and hope to frighten it off?

The uncertainty was fraying her nerves. Deciding it was better to know what she was up against, she switched on her flashlight. The strong beam pierced the empty darkness.

'Stephanie?'

She couldn't have imagined how pleased she'd be to hear William's voice. He emerged into the light, stumbling with the awkwardness of an armful of something unknown. He dropped the bundle, fished in a pocket for his own flashlight and directed it on to her face.

'Are you all right?' he asked, kneeling beside her.

Sheer relief loosened her tongue. 'I thought it was a wild animal because I couldn't see a light — how did you find your way back without using your flashlight?'

'With difficulty, I can tell you. I needed both hands . . . for carrying things.' His voice deepened. 'But how are you?'

'A little cold, and you are right, it could get worse before it gets better.'

Stephanie got up from her cramped position and used her foot to turn over whatever he had found in the shepherds' hut. It was a pile of skins, sheep or goat. She couldn't tell which and it didn't matter. They were animal.

She had never smelled anything like it. She wrinkled her nose in the darkness. How had he carried them all the way up the mountain without being overcome? It was a marathon effort for which she had to give him full marks.

'So, you've found something?' she asked, trying not to show her distaste, knowing she should be grateful.

William laughed. 'Something? A good word, that. Not very sanitised, I'm afraid, but it's a covering we'll be glad of later.' He shook out three or four skins, then, taking his coat off Ross, laid the skins across the prone body. 'And how has our patient been?'

'He's hardly moved, but his hand is quite warm. Your coat kept his body temperature up.' A thought occurred to Stephanie. 'How did you manage without it?'

William shrugged himself back into his coat before he answered. 'Mountain climbing is invigorating, let me tell you.'

She felt a stab of contrition. It was a big thing she had asked of him.

'William, I'm most appreciative of what you have done and are doing. It's far beyond the call of duty, as they say, for an authority on wildflowers.'

He came to stand close to her, so close she would feel his warm breath on her cold face 'Stephanie, there's something . . . ' He stared at her in the glow from her torch and began again. 'Stephanie, I should . . . '

He broke off with a muttered exclamation and turned away to survey the site with his flashlight. When he spoke again it was in a matter-of-fact voice. 'I couldn't carry enough skins to cover three bodies properly and there's not room for both of us next to Ross. If you and I are to share, we'll need to find somewhere more comfortable.

Stephanie was so cold and tired her heart didn't miss a beat at William's suggested arrangements. In fact, she would have agreed to sit down next to the Devil if it meant being warm.

No warning bells sounded as she watched him choose a sheltered position up against a boulder within calling distance if Ross should come round and need them. A sheepskin, fleece-side up, was laid on the ground. Good idea, she thought, massaging the effects of sitting on the rough hillside for however long it was that William had been away.

She flopped down on to the skin's softness with a long exhalation of breath. It certainly felt good.

'It doesn't smell too bad,' she reported, wanting to believe it.

That made William laugh. 'That's

what I like about you Australians, always optimistic. Doesn't anything get you down?'

Stephanie knew the answer to that — people like Marion, the dog-lover, and now Ross, who couldn't be told anything, got her down. But, as the tour leader, she couldn't admit to such feelings, not even to a fellow employee of *Far Corners Travel*.

'They breed them tough in Australia,' she joked as he sat down beside her.

He spread skins across their feet, legs and laps. As the full length of his body pressed up against her side, she wondered how long it would be before help came. It was going to be hard to remain impersonal in such an intimate situation. And keep up the impression of optimism.

'I spoke too soon about the smell,' she said, nervously.

There was still a trace of humour in his voice when he answered her. 'Indeed. And the warmth of our bodies will . . . ' He paused to think of a suitable word. 'Shall we say, enhance the aroma?'

That was her answer — she would be able to get through a close encounter with the plant specialist if she kept it humorous. They obviously had a similar sense of the ridiculous.

It was easier to think that than to carry it out. William's arm reached behind her to draw her closer. After the initial shock and instinctive withdrawal, Stephanie decided it was very comfortable sitting that way. In fact, it was comforting as well. In a friendly way, of course. She was surprised how much she needed the comfort of a friend. She turned her head to say so.

'It really is — '

'Are you all — '

They both spoke at the same time.

'After you,' William said.

'No, what were you going to say?'

'Ladies first, Stephanie.'

'It was nothing. Well, it was something. I really appreciate you doing this.'

'Enough said. You've already thanked me. Now, it's probably going to be a long wait, so why don't you put your head on my shoulder and try and sleep?' The arm across her shoulders tightened and pulled her towards him.

It seemed like a very good idea. The warmth generated by their bodies was already having its effect — her head felt heavy, her eyelids droopy. She gave way and relaxed. They were a perfect fit and, up close, the familiar fresh smell of his aftershave won out against the rankness of the skins. With a tiny sigh, she snuggled under his chin and drifted . . .

Stephanie was suddenly wide awake. Had she dreamed William's head was resting on hers? No, it wasn't a dream, she could feel its weight. Had he fallen asleep, too?

'I thought I told you to go to sleep,' he murmured without moving. Almost as if he was in charge.

How could he tell she was staring into the darkness? Did that mean he could also feel her dismay at the reversal of their roles? She wanted to get on safer ground — but how?

'Tell me about yourself.' It was almost another order. And despite her resolution to take back control of the situation, that was what she did.

She told him about the happy, secure country-town upbringing that gave her the confidence to become a flight attendant with a national airline. And about its collapse.

'Is there a significant other in your life?'

A significant other? What made William ask that? Stephanie realised her world had narrowed down to the tour and she had forgotten Martin, steady, reliable Martin. He was like a memory, a distant memory of another time, no longer a significant other.

As she searched for a suitable answer, she felt William stiffen.

'Someone's coming!'

Stephanie peered into the darkness. A cavalcade of lanterns and powerful lights was moving up the mountainside, cheerful male voices echoing on the night air.

'Switch on your torch,' William suggested. 'It'll help them locate us.' He got to his feet and shouted, 'Over here!'

Left sitting among the smelly skins, Stephanie was surprised by disappointment, not sure she wanted to be found just yet. Reminding herself that Ross needed help, she stood up and added another beacon of light to guide the rescuers.

The group was already assembled in the breakfast room when Stephanie came down the next morning. With one exception — William. That was not surprising; she'd found it difficult to get out of bed herself, every muscle complaining at being asked to go into action so soon after the gruelling hours on the mountain.

On the way through the room to join Yanni, she stopped to speak to each table. There wasn't one complaint, only interest in how the misadventure had left Ross. She glossed over the struggle to stretcher him down to the road and the hours spent in the hospital emergency ward until he was settled.

The head waiter had seen her enter and hurried forward with a pot of tea as soon as she sat down. The hotel cat brushed up against her legs. Everything was reassuringly normal.

'I have been in touch with the hospital — ' Yanni reported.

'Already?'

He grinned. 'We Greeks start work early, remember.'

'Even after a late night?'

'Especially after a late night. We do not bother going to bed.'

Stephanie laughed at that, then became business-like.

'What time are they expecting the Medical Evacuation team, Yanni?' she asked.

'This morning. They are already in Athens. Do not worry, there is nothing more we need to do. Ross will be back in Australia in no time.'

'I should like to go and see him before we set out for the walk today.'

Yanni nodded absently. 'We can do that. But there is another thing.' He paused for so long Stephanie became impatient.

'Go on, Yanni, tell me. It can't be any worse than what we've been through.'

His face was grave. 'It is about William.'

Stephanie suddenly felt apprehensive.

'Last night at the hospital . . . ' Yanni was looking everywhere but at her. 'I have seen a lot of summer love. It will pass. But you must be careful. It would not be good for the clients to find out . . . not the Pearsons.'

Stephanie couldn't keep the astonishment from her voice. 'Summer love?' She almost shouted the words, her face pink with indignation. 'Whatever are you talking about?'

Yanni was looking at her, frowning a warning. She turned her head; Harriet Pearson had come up behind her unnoticed.

'Such rosy cheeks after such a long night! I am surprised. I expected you'd be looking all washed out. But tell me, is Ross all right? And where is William?' Harriet asked.

Yanni rose from his seat. 'Ross is comfortable, Harriet. If you will excuse me, ladies, I have duties to perform. His belongings need to be packed.'

Stephanie's heart sank. Harriet was the last person she wanted to talk to right then. She wanted to detain Yanni, tell him how wrong he was to assume she had special feelings for William. And to ask him how he came to such a silly conclusion. After all, they had been thrown together by unfortunate circumstances.

'I'm glad William isn't down yet, I want to talk to you alone, Stephanie,' Harriet said. 'You know how Sue and I were sure William isn't who he says he is?'

Yanni was right about one thing. She had to be careful with the Pearsons. If, like him, they got the wrong idea and thought there was a relationship between William and herself, they wouldn't let up.

William had jokingly referred to them as ferrets; it was proving apt; Harriet was nothing if not persistent, determined to find out whatever she could.

And, if thwarted, would her rage extend to complaining about it to *Far Corners Travel* on their return to Australia? There was nothing between William and her that needed reporting but even the suggestion could mean her job.

'Well,' Harriet drew out the word, to make sure of Stephanie's attention, then went on. 'We asked my daughter-in-law to do some enquiring on the Internet. She knows how to do these things better than Sue and I.'

Stephanie had to ask herself was the woman mad? Or just couldn't bear to be bested? What was the saying, hell hath no fury like a woman scorned? It didn't matter that William hadn't scorned the Pearsons, just avoided their obvious advances.

At least, she understood that was what had happened. Was she being naïve? Had it been more than that? Had William encouraged Sue? And then tired of the game?

'It seems we were right!' Harriet paused for effect, triumph blazing in her eyes. 'He's supposed to be a plant specialist from Kew Gardens, but there's no such person there.'

Stephanie couldn't think of a thing to say. Harriet's information drove thoughts of Yanni's mistake from her mind, and filled it with new questions.

Could it be true? For all she knew, William could have conned the travel company to get the job. On the mountain the night before, she'd learned nothing about him; their talk had been all about her. Would he have told her something of himself if the rescuers hadn't arrived when they did?

And, if she'd thought to let him,

instead of talking her head off about herself.

'You'll have to ask to see his passport now, won't you, Stephanie?' Harriet went on, relentlessly.

At the monastery at Preveli, Yanni gathered the group around the fountain. It was donated by an Australian as a memorial to the bravery of the monks and local villagers who sheltered Allied soldiers from the enemy after the Battle of Crete was lost in 1941.

'You remember the old man we met on the mountain who told us about his father hiding the soldiers?' He pointed across the cobbled courtyard. 'Below the cliffs over there is the bay where the submarines came in to take them away to Cairo. Come and look.'

'It's interesting to hear some recent history in this land of antiquities, isn't it?' Tom Gleeson remarked to Stephanie as they walked across.

There were no wildflowers within the stone walls of the monastery, only the raised beds where the monks grew their vegetables, and no need for William's expertise. Yet to her surprise, he took over from Yanni.

He invited the group to lean over the parapet and check out the height of the steep cliffs and the difficult donkey track that led down to the bay.

'The soldiers were rescued from under the nose of the enemy, first in small boats and later in submarines. Eventually. the monastery came under suspicion and was occupied. The Allies in Cairo decided the Abbot had to be rescued.'

Stephanie listened in admiration. William spoke with confidence, easily holding the group's interest. He seemed to know his subject well, expanding the story with details of naval movements of the time.

It was a polished performance and didn't fit in with her idea of a plant man at all. More like a teacher, or a lecturer.

Harriet Pearson's accusations surfaced again. Although she'd managed to put the woman off in the orderly confusion of organising the day's outing, the question remained. It was hard not to ask it now.

If William wasn't a wildflower expert, who was he?

9

Stephanie's strides slowed as the road up the hill to the old fort and the Naval Museum became steeper. Determined to give her legs a good work-out before the long, cramped flight from Greece back to Australia, she was pushing herself beyond her usual limits.

She paused as she reached the top to take one last look out over the entrance to the harbour and to gratefully fill her straining lungs with sea air. Although her heart was pounding and her leg muscles protesting, she felt a sense of satisfaction.

Beyond the actual pleasure of physical exertion there was another reason for her feeling of well-being. She knew that when the *Walk on the Wild Side* tour ended later that day she could take some pride in its success.

She had kept her head when Ross

had his accident, and even curbed Marion's habit of feeding stray dogs. And now, with only one day to go, it seemed she had managed to quieten the Pearson women — by refusing their demands for action over William an embarrassing showdown had been avoided.

Her own interest in who he really was had been overtaken by the pressure of providing the *Far Corners* clients with a Greek experience to remember. There hadn't been time for idle speculation.

There was no sign of tourists as she strode on down the winding streets; it was too early for them. The boutique shops were shuttered, still closed after late shopping the night before. Her light footfalls barely disturbed the early morning stillness that lay over the whole area.

Stephanie took a break when she reached the deserted residential street that would lead her back to the harbour and to the hotel, hopefully refreshed and ready for the long day ahead. She perched on a low wall and reached for the water bottle that hung from her waist, upended it and quenched her thirst.

Half-way down the street, a bright blue door opened and a man stepped out, pausing to carefully pull it closed behind him. Without looking around, he set off down the street in the direction of the harbour, a shaft of early morning sun catching his fair hair as he turned a corner and disappeared.

Stephanie's heart missed a beat. What was William doing coming from a house at this hour of the day? Almost as if it was a familiar routine. Once again, the doubts, first raised by Harriet and Sue, but put aside as being no business of hers, reminded her how little she knew about him.

They had worked together on a daily basis and yet nothing about his private life had emerged. She knew that had been because she hadn't asked, determined not to indulge in the Pearsons' flights of fancy. And to be business-like.

William had obviously felt the same. Even during their night on the mountainside with the injured Ross, when she had talked about her life back in Australia, William had offered no insight into his own. She still felt a little embarrassed at how self-centred that must've seemed to him at the time.

That is, unless keeping her talking about herself had been a deliberate ploy because he had something to hide, a secret life in a hideaway in a back street.

A sudden random recollection of William flashed through her mind. It was the day of the lunch with Fiona, the travel agent, when she had seen him in earnest conversation in a dark café in these very streets.

Was he involved in something shady? Had be been making deals? If so, what kind of deals would a wildflower expert be making?

When the answer came to her, Stephanie wondered why she hadn't thought of it sooner. If William had spent the night in this house in this street, there must be a secret somebody who lived behind the blue door.

She wasn't prepared for the wave of gut-wrenching pain that shook her. What was happening to her? Why was she so upset? William's actions were nothing to do with her.

It was hard to accept, but why should he be any different to the hundreds of holiday-makers who came to Greece each year and found a summer love? As far as she knew, he was free to do so.

As far as she knew! That was it. She reminded herself she knew nothing about him, other than that he was handsome and charming. They had worked well together and she'd enjoyed his company . . . as a colleague. Nothing more.

Even as she reassured herself another sickening thought came to mind. Had she, like the Pearsons, made more of his attention, and, without admitting it to herself, come to believe there was something special between them? And this was jealousy that was clawing at her?

Dismayed by the thought and unable to trust her legs to carry her, she stayed where she was, gazing down the now-empty street, wondering if she'd only imagined it was William she'd seen.

With trembling hands, she lifted the water bottle to her mouth again and emptied it with great gulps in an attempt to calm her turbulent feelings. And make some sense of them.

Stephanie had no idea how long it was that she sat there before she became aware of footsteps echoing down the cobbled laneways and dark figures drifting across her line of vision. The working day had begun for the residents of Chania. And for herself. Somehow she had to get through the day as if nothing had happened. Especially in front of William.

She got up and turned in the direction of the hotel.

★ ★ ★

The ocean drive to Iraklion was one of wild beauty, but Stephanie scarcely noticed the scenery. She sat unseeing beside Yanni in the front of the comfortable coach.

With the organising of their departure from the hotel over, there was nothing to occupy her mind. Behind her, she could hear the low murmur of the unusually subdued voices of members of the group.

That morning several of them had expressed their regret at reaching the end of the tour, but Stephanie's feelings were mixed. Part of her wanted it to be over, so that she could return to her normal life and begin putting behind her what could only be called a summer madness.

But another part of her wished it could go on forever. She lifted her eyes to the large rear-vision mirror above Costas' head. The cause of her conflict was leaning across the aisle, referring to a book on his knees, conversing with the Gillespies.

As if suddenly aware of her scrutiny, William turned his head and stared back at her.

A mild panic gripped her. He couldn't know how she felt about him, could he? She hadn't until that morning, when the shock of seeing him in the old town had unmasked her feelings for him. Had she unwittingly given herself away?

She recalled the effort it had taken to go into the breakfast room on her return to the hotel earlier. And to act normally.

It hadn't been helped by Harriet choosing that moment to make a last minute attempt to be proven right. Standing in the foyer, checking suitcases ready for departure, Stephanie wondered at the woman's sense of timing.

'Well, have you asked William who he is, yet?' Harriet had demanded belligerently.

Interrupted in her counting, Stephanie threw up her arms. 'It's not a good time, Harriet,' she replied as pleasantly as she could.

'Does that mean you haven't?'

Stephanie stared at the woman. Why was it so important? It no longer mattered who William was; the tour was almost over. She wondered how Harriet would react if she told her what she'd seen that morning in the old town. And how she felt about him.

'I think you'll agree William has done a good job,' she had answered, turning away from the angry woman and beginning her count again.

In the rear-vision mirror, William held her gaze for a long moment then the beginnings of a smile tugged at the corners of his mouth and spread.

Stephanie felt herself responding . . . until a wayward image of the little house with a blue door in a back street superimposed itself on her mind. Abruptly, she turned her head away.

The coached slowed. Surprised at how quickly they had reached their first destination for the day, Stephanie took up the microphone, and, standing in the aisle, faced the group.

'Wake up, folks!' she teased. 'In case there are those of you who may have forgotten, I'll run through the arrangements again. Firstly, we'll be taken on a tour of the Palace of Knossos. Afterwards, it's only a short drive to a hotel where we'll have lunch and freshen up before making our way to the airport.'

10

The coach had come to a halt at the end of a long line of stationary vehicles that snaked out of sight around a bend in the road. Dismayed, she gave Yanni a distracted glance before going on.

'This is obviously a very popular place for visitors,' she said, 'so we'll need to stay together. I wouldn't like to lose any one of you at this late stage.'

She slipped back into her seat beside Yanni. He was frowning. 'We are not near Knossos yet,' he informed her, and leaned forward to exchange words in Greek with the driver.

Although she didn't understand what was being said, Stephanie felt a prickle of foreboding. The day needed to run like clockwork if they were to fly to Athens and connect with the onward flight to Australia.

'I am going to find out what is

happening,' Yanni said. He stepped down from the coach and was immediately lost in the crowd of anxious drivers swarming the road.

Stephanie wasn't sure if Athens airport was more chaotic than she remembered or if it just seemed so, given her level of anxiety.

On her arrival two weeks ago, she'd been stressed out over her new job and thought her suitcase was being stolen. Now, she welcomed the sights and sounds of disorder, thankful they had reached it in time.

The carefully planned day had disintegrated into a nightmare of rearranged schedules because of the rockfall on the road to Iraklion that took hours to clear. Many of the smaller vehicles in the miles of banked-up traffic were able to turn, to go back the way they came and find a detour.

The narrowness of the road at that particular point meant Costas was unable to do the same with the coach, and they were trapped.

Still marvelling at having made the check-in at all, Stephanie shepherded her group towards the first of the security gates. There was a round of farewells as Yanni was left at the barrier.

At last it was her turn. 'Thank you for all your help, Yanni,' she said. 'I couldn't have managed without you.'

He shrugged expressively. 'Now you are experienced, perhaps you will be given the Sites of Antiquity tour later in the year and be back here soon,' he suggested. 'But, if not, I will expect you this time next year, yes?'

'I should be so lucky,' she replied, through the beginnings of tears. 'I'm on a single contract, you know, and the accident to Ross might go against me.'

Yanni looked as if he was about to say something then changed his mind. Instead, he surprised her by gripping her shoulders and kissing her on both cheeks, a departure from the formal behaviour he'd shown her throughout the tour. It made leaving even harder.

'Do not worry, he will get over it,'

was all he said, waving her towards the metal detectors.

At first Stephanie thought he'd made a mistake with his English. Dismayed that Yanni still believed she had feelings for William and would think less of her, she wanted to explain.

She needed to tell him that until today she'd been unaware of the attraction, but he had already turned away. There was one last glimpse of the familiar figure before he was lost in the crowd.

'Very touching,' said a voice behind her. 'A summer love, perhaps?'

Harriet Pearson had been standing inside the barrier, watching.

Stephanie caught her bottom lip between her teeth, refusing to be drawn into a denial. The woman really did try her patience!

'The Greek people are warm and friendly, don't you agree, Harriet?' she said. Without waiting for a reply, she looked about her. 'Now, where is everybody? I see our flight is boarding.'

As they moved down the concourse towards the departure lounges she could see William ahead. The fact that for the first time in two weeks he would not be coming with them, had become reality. Passengers for his flight to London would be gathering in another departure lounge.

He was leaving and neither she or the Pearson women were any closer to knowing the truth about him. It no longer mattered.

She quickened her steps, telling herself she just wanted to thank him for the way he had filled the long hours of waiting by the roadside.

He had led the group on an exploration of a nearby gorge, and even found a wayside café that served coffee and baklava. They had returned to the coach clutching bouquets of aromatic wild herbs. There was no doubt it had lessened some of the disappointment they felt at having to bypass Knosses.

'I wanted to thank you for everything and especially for today,' she said when she reached him.

'Stephanie! I've been looking for you,' he said, reaching out to draw her aside from the steady stream of passengers. 'There's something I want to tell you.'

'I wasn't going to go without saying goodbye,' she assured him, her breath catching in her throat at the thought.

'But, is it to be goodbye?' William's voice was low, barely audible above the noise of the airport.

Stephanie gave him a startled glance. Had she heard him right? What else could it be except goodbye?

'Sorry?'

William leaned closer, the remembered fresh smell of his aftershave teasing her nostrils. 'Does it have to be goodbye?' he asked in her ear.

Of course, it had to be goodbye, they were going in opposite directions. In six or seven hours he would be back in England, in twenty-four, she would be in Australia.

'The tour is over, William,' she

replied, her voice wobbling as she tried to hide her emotion.

'Yes, but this isn't,' he murmured.

His move to separate her from the passing crowds brought her back hard up against the plate-glass wall behind her. That pushed her cabin-bag around to the front of her body. As the strap slipped down off her shoulder and into the crook of her arm it jerked the bag against his knee.

Apologising, Stephanie awkwardly juggled her business satchel under the other arm and made a futile, one-handed grab to hoist the shoulder-bag up again. William reached out to help her. It brought him too close for comfort, her comfort.

She was pinned to the wall with nowhere to go. 'I have to . . . the group . . . ' she stammered.

'Stephanie, the group has set the agenda for two weeks,' he said. 'Isn't it time we did what we want? As you correctly informed me not two minutes ago, the tour is over.'

It didn't make sense. She knew she'd strictly adhered to the rules, but was William saying he had done the same? Against his feelings? She stared at him.

As she hesitated, he inclined his head until his lips were on hers. For one mad moment, she forgot who and where she was and welcomed his kiss. She tightened her hold on her business satchel, fighting the longing to drop it, too, so as to leave her arms free to wind around his neck.

'So this is why you wouldn't check out this man's true identity!'

11

Harriet Pearson's strident accusation cut through Stephanie's moment of mindless pleasure. She drew back from William in dismay. That this fall from grace, after two weeks of exemplary behaviour, should be witnessed by Harriet of all people, was disastrous.

She was acutely aware of William's hand on her arm; he hadn't taken it away when Harriet began her tirade. No doubt he meant it to be comforting, a sign of solidarity, but she thought it was likely to further inflame the Pearsons.

Already shaken by her response to his kiss and what it might have revealed, she tried to unobtrusively shake it off by changing her hand-luggage from one position to another.

It didn't work. With his hand still on her arm, William faced the two women as if he had nothing to hide.

Nothing to hide? He was good at that. How could she have forgotten the house in the back street in Chania? Did one kiss wipe that out? The answer was yes.

'It must be against company policy for one thing,' Harriet went on, her glittering eyes reflecting her frustration. 'I'm sure they'll be interested in how you put your pleasure before the wishes of your clients.'

Sue Pearson had come to stand behind her mother. Stephanie looked at her hoping she would persuade Harriet to back off and prevent an ugly scene. But this pursuit of William had obviously escalated into an obsession for her.

Stephanie knew some mother-daughter relationships could be tricky, but if this was how Sue allowed her mother to run her romantic life it was no wonder she was in her late thirties and still single.

'You're wrong, Harriet,' she began, diplomatically and truthfully, without looking at William. After all, it was his fault this had happened — if he hadn't kissed her . . .

'Ours has been nothing more than a working relationship, which I hope has resulted in a more enjoyable tour for you,' she went on.

Harriet was not to be mollified. 'You don't deny that there would be a clause in your contract forbidding it?'

'Well, no, there isn't a specific — '

'Harriet!' interrupted William. 'Before you even think of causing trouble for Stephanie, who, by the way, has worked untiringly for you, there is something you should know.'

Behind William's tight smile and silky-smooth voice Stephanie detected a hint of menace. Harriet Pearson obviously sensed it, too, and took an involuntary step backwards.

After all, what did either of them know about him? Rightly or wrongly, that had been Harriet's complaint. Nothing had changed.

But could this well-spoken, charming

man turn nasty? No, Stephanie wouldn't believe that, but clearly Harriet was having her doubts. And William was certainly giving notice he would stand no more nonsense from the Pearsons.

He went on. 'I am no longer under contract to *Far Corners Travel*. My responsibilities ended this morning at breakfast. In that case, you'll agree I can say goodbye to whomever I like, however I like. And I say goodbye to you and your lovely daughter with pleasure. In my view, you have behaved abominably.'

The Pearsons looked shocked. Before they could recover their equilibrium there was a burst of unintelligible announcements over the loudspeakers.

William's grip on Stephanie's arm loosened. 'That's the last call for my flight,' he said, his face unreadable. 'I have to go now.'

He turned, and without a backward glance, hurried away.

12

Back in Australia two days later, Stephanie made her way through the park towards the *Far Corners Travel* offices. A sharp wind whistled up from the river. It shook the autumn leaves from the trees that lined the wide path. They littered the ground below, making work for the approaching motorised street-sweeper.

She clutched her coat collar more tightly around her throat as it passed and thought longingly of the heavily-scented orange trees in the streets near the tour hotel in Athens, of the meadows of spring wildflowers in Crete, and the promise of long, hot summer days to come.

With a twinge of guilt she pushed open the glass door at *Far Corners Travel* and took the lift to the first floor.

She had broken the unwritten rule not to become personally involved with anyone on the tour, but she wasn't going to admit to it; there was no need. It was over.

Before it started, as it happened. William had made that clear, hurrying off to catch his plane without another word, leaving the Pearsons and herself speechless. It was she who recovered first — she had a job to do, and, unlike William, her contract extended to escorting the clients back to Australia.

Jean, her supervisor, looked up from her desk to greet her as she emerged from the lift.

'Stephanie, you made it! And from all accounts, you did well.'

'It was not without its drama, I'm afraid,' Stephanie answered ruefully, shedding her coat and sitting down. 'Do I have to fill out any more forms?'

'No, the e-mail you sent from Chania covered everything. Just bad luck. The insurance people have paid without a murmur, Ross is OK — ?'

'I don't want to hear that man's name ever again!'

'Nothing further to report?' Jean gave her a penetrating look. 'No summer love?'

Stephanie glared back indignantly. 'And if I hear that phrase once more, I'll . . . '

'You'll what?' Jean teased her. 'Tell the truth? No-one goes to Greece without falling in love.'

Stephanie quickly recovered her good humour. 'I must admit I did fall in love . . . ' She paused for maximum effect, smiling as Jean's face lit up in anticipation. 'With Greece.'

Jean laughed. 'I asked for that, didn't I?' She shuffled through the papers on her desk and picked out a letter. 'How did you get on with Harriet Pearson?'

Stephanie's heart sank. It had been too much to expect Harriet wouldn't complain and report her suspicions about Stephanie and Yanni. Had the woman gone even further in her vindictiveness and given *Far Corners*

Travel her full version of their employee's behaviour? Or had William silenced her?

Certainly, after the angry William had answered the last boarding call for his flight and disappeared, the Pearson women had very little to say. Almost meekly, they had followed the other members of the group through the last of the security procedures and on to the plane.

'She accused me of having a relationship with Yanni. And questioned William's identity,' she said, hoping that was the full extent of the complaint.

Jean nodded as it if was no surprise. Stephanie waited to hear more. If Harriet was correct, perhaps now her boss would explain if William wasn't who he said he was. Or rather, who Far Corners claimed he was.

'I was able to assure her we were happy with his credentials,' was all Jean said.

Stephanie wished someone would do the same for her, instead of leaving her with only the memory of the painful scene at Athens Airport. And unanswered questions. Harriet's interruption had blown away any chance of hearing an explanation from him. That is, if he had intended to give her one.

And even now she couldn't ask Jean, however casually, what those credentials were, not without revealing how close she'd come to breaking the rules.

And her interest in the answer. Jean clipped the correspondence together and stowed it in a folder with an air of finality. 'Now, let's talk about your next assignment. Are you ready for another?'

Stephanie had no idea where the decision came from, when the need to know became compelling. What had William meant in those few moments before Harriet found them? Was she the only one who felt the connection between them when they kissed?

Or had she just imagined it? There hadn't been a chance to find out.

It was clear Jean wasn't going to volunteer any further information, and

Stephanie had to admit it was likely her boss wouldn't have the answers she needed, anyway. She'd have to ask them herself.

She stood up. 'Not just yet, if you don't mind, Jean. I have to go to London on business.'

The house wasn't hard to find. Like others in the street, it stood back from the road in quite a large garden. A tasteful board on one gatepost bore the name, *Elysium*.

The gates were open on to a gravel driveway, but Stephanie resisted the invitation to drive in; it seemed a little overconfident and that was the last thing she felt. There were questions she'd come a long way to ask, answers to which might or might not please her.

She parked the rental car and walked the short distance to the handsome, two-storied house. The garden was of extraordinary diversity and beauty, which shouldn't have been a surprise; the English were famous for their gardens and William was a plant man.

And the name on the gate should've prepared her — it was a Greek word that meant Paradise.

She rang the doorbell, heard it echoing behind the solid door. As she waited, a sudden rush of apprehension left her weak-kneed. What a mad idea coming to England had been!

It had seemed so simple back in Australia — just go to London and ask William who he was and what she meant to him. If she meant anything at all. There was always a risk she didn't.

But, now she was at his door, she wondered what would he think of her action? That she was as bad as the Pearson women, blatantly pursuing him? He could.

Had she only imagined there was something special between them, were her feelings just a burst of last-minute emotion on parting? Or was it the much-derided summer love?

Stephanie no longer felt able to either ask those questions or accept the answers. She wondered was she suffering jet-lag;

she knew it affected different people differently.

The idea grew in her mind that she should go away now and come back another day, if ever, when she'd be better able to cope.

Yes, she decided, it was time to leave.

Dismissing the suspicion she'd simply lost her nerve, and, eager to put the decision into action, she stepped away from the door and faced the driveway. It was all she could do not to break into a run.

It was too late. Behind her, she heard the door open and a voice call, 'May I help you?'

She stopped and turned. A woman stood in the doorway. Stephanie quickly decided she was too old to be William's wife. That came as a relief — a wife was someone she foolishly hadn't contemplated. Should she have? After all, he hadn't worn a wedding ring.

'I've come to see William.'

The woman said nothing, eyebrows

raised expectantly, obviously waiting for more details.

'The people at Kew sent me,' Stephanie went on, gaining a little confidence, remembering the difficulties she'd encountered. 'There was trouble with the name. I thought it was just Brown, not Cunningham-Browne, which explains why Harriet couldn't trace him. It took forever to sort.'

She knew by the woman's puzzled face she was talking in riddles, but, having started, couldn't stop herself.

'But, once we got over that hurdle, they were happy to give me this address. And the directions, of course.'

The explanation seemed to satisfy the woman. 'I'm Felicity Cunningham-Browne. Won't you come in?' she invited.

Stephanie felt another jolt at the name. Did William live with his mother? Or was this William's wife, after all.

Up close, it was hard to tell the woman's age. The heart-shaped face was smooth and unlined, not like the sun-coarsened skin of Australian women.

Felicity Cunningham-Browne led the way down a hallway to a bright room that opened out on to a back garden as beautiful as the front. A man sat in a wheelchair in the sunlight, one plaster-encased leg stretched out in front of him.

Stephanie drew in her breath. William had been injured! When had that happened? It was only ten days since they parted in Athens. With an effort, she stifled the impulse to hurry to his side.

'William, someone to see you,' Felicity announced.

The wheelchair swung round. An older version of William faced Stephanie. The vivid blue eyes were the same, with the same laughter-lines at the corners, but etched more deeply by time. The hair was thinner and, although some of its brilliance had faded, was still fair.

'And what can I do for you, young lady?'

'I came to see William,' she stammered, startled by the likeness.

The laughter-lines became more marked as the smile reached his eyes. 'I am he.'

Stephanie had heard those same words uttered, in the same tones, early one morning in a hotel doorway in Athens.

Behind her, Felicity laughed. 'Oh, you're looking for our son! I thought you must've been a student of William's, but I should've guessed you weren't by the Australian accent. He doesn't often have girls chasing him up, do you, William?'

Chasing him? Although it was put in a joking manner, the remark embarrassed Stephanie. How many times had his family answered the door to young women looking for their son?

She could feel the deep blush as it rose from her throat and enveloped her face. She definitely should not have come! She backed away, wanting to get out of the house as soon as possible.

'We call him Will,' explained Felicity,

hardly noticing she had blocked off Stephanie's escape route. 'Now, sit down and talk to William whilst I make us some tea. You must be thirsty if you've come over from Kew. All that traffic!' She disappeared.

Stephanie found herself a seat opposite the man in the wheelchair.

'Now, tell me, what brings you here?' he asked with an achingly familiar, attentive look.

'I'm with *Far Corners Travel* — '

'Aah, yes, *Far Corners*. I did feel bad about the accident, but Will suggested to the company that we keep faith with them by going himself. He really is an historian but knows a lot about my work. Naturally.'

Stephanie marvelled at the simple explanation. No mystery, no drama, just a broken ankle and a historian son offering to fulfil his father's commitment.

'He insisted on changing his name, though, afraid people would think he was me and expect him to know it all.'

William Cunningham-Browne senior chuckled. 'And he wouldn't wear the hyphenated name, anyway. He said Australians would call it double-barrelled and take the . . . what would you call it, the mickey out of him.'

He leaned forward. 'Would you have?' he asked.

Suddenly at ease with the charming man, Stephanie agreed. 'Most definitely, although that's probably not how we would describe it.'

There was a slight rattle of crockery as Felicity wheeled the tea-trolley into the room. She poured tea into cups of delicate bone china and handed one to Stephanie.

Having passed a cup to William, then taken one for herself, Felicity sat down and addressed her husband.

'Well, William, were you able to help this young woman?'

He gave Stephanie a helpless look that once again reminded her of his son. 'I'm sorry, I forgot what you were asking.'

'I came to see William, I mean, Will. Is he at home?'

'You must have misunderstood him,' Felicity answered. 'He doesn't live here but after William had his accident, he was popping in as often as possible. Just to see everything was all right. Which of course, it was. So there was no need to hurry back from Greece.' She smiled fondly. 'But he did.'

'I assured him these things just take time,' added her husband.

Stephanie felt as if she was losing the plot. She directed a shaft of righteous anger at the absent William for the embarrassing position she was in.

Why couldn't he have at least told her that much about himself instead of nothing? Hadn't he trusted her? After all, they had been on the same side!

But, sitting drinking tea with this charming couple wasn't answering her questions. Only William was able to do that.

'Could you direct me to where he

lives?' she asked as patiently as she could.

'That wouldn't do any good, he's not there,' said William's father, carefully dunking a digestive biscuit in his tea. 'He has gone to Australia.'

13

Stephanie was bewildered. More than ever convinced she was suffering from jet-lag, she struggled to make sense of what William's father was saying.

'Australia? Why would he go there? Were you booked for another tour?' Even as she asked, she knew that William couldn't be deputising for his father this time; it was almost winter in Australia, not the season for wild-flowers.

William Cunningham-Browne senior didn't seem to notice anything strange about her behaviour.

'We didn't ask why he was going,' he said, holding out his cup for a refill. 'He could see we were getting along fine and he hadn't needed to hurry home.'

At last something made sense to Stephanie. Could William's anxiety to get back to his parents explain his abrupt, almost rude, farewell at Athens Airport?

'It is probably something to do with his book,' Felicity offered.

'His book?' Stephanie was back in unknown territory.

'He's writing a book about the 1939-45 war and the occupation of Crete during that time,' Felicity explained proudly. 'That's one of the reasons he was able to take William's place. He knows Crete so well.'

Another piece of the puzzle clicked into place for Stephanie. That would explain how he was able to speak with such authority the day the group went to Preveli Monastery; he knew the story of the escaping Allied servicemen.

She wondered would his parents think she was dumb if she asked another question. She decided to risk it.

'But didn't you say he has gone to Australia?'

'Yes.' Felicity poured a second cup of tea for her husband and passed it over.

'That was what he said. Another cup, Stephanie?'

★   ★   ★

There was something of the Mad Hatter's tea party about the scene, Stephanie told her mother by phone later that evening.

'There we were, the three of us, drinking tea and talking at cross-purposes. Unreal.'

'There's nothing unreal about him writing a book, Stephanie. When you weren't here he said he was going to get on with it.'

'He said? What do you mean?' asked Stephanie, unable to believe what she was hearing. 'Did you see him?'

'Yes, he came here,' replied her mother, as if a visitor from England was an everyday thing.

Stephanie's mind was grappling with the new revelations. And their possible meaning. 'Did you tell him where I was?'

'No, dear, I wasn't sure I should. You had never mentioned any particular man. He could have been anybody.' Anne Turner managed to sound self-righteous and concerned at the same time.

But that was it, William wasn't just anybody; Stephanie knew she wouldn't have gone to this much trouble for just anybody, but her mother didn't.

'Martin agreed I did the right thing.'

Stephanie was dismayed. 'Martin was there when he came?'

She wondered what William had made of that. Had it given him the wrong idea? She was suddenly reminded of their conversation during the night on the mountain.

He had asked was there a significant other in her life. Had he been interested then or just making conversation? The arrival of the rescuers had meant she hadn't needed to answer.

As she hung up the phone, Stephanie wished her mother had been more forthcoming to the stranger at her door.

After all, he had crossed half the world.

Just as she had, to see him.

More pieces of the jigsaw fell into place. As she picked up the phone again, Stephanie smiled to herself.

14

Stephanie paid off the taxi in the car-park behind the hotel in Chania and pulled her trolley-case down an alley-way out on to the harbour front. Holidaying crowds thronged the cobbled streets of the wild town, revelling in the heat. The tavernas along the quays were packed. It was summer, the height of the season.

She wondered how many of the young women coming to Greece dreamed of a summer love. She hadn't, just the opposite. In fact, she hadn't known such a state existed, and when told of it, had scoffed at the idea of falling in love in Greece. But it had happened.

Now she had to find out if it was something lasting, not just a holiday romance.

It was cool inside the hotel. Eleni, the

owner, came from behind her desk with a welcoming embrace. And a non-stop flow of comments.

'Stephanie! How good to see you again! Come and sit down,' she said, taking Stephanie's trolley-case and stowing it. 'You have come to see William, yes? It is no good expecting him just yet, he and Yanni are out all day interviewing the old men in the mountain villages. For his book, you know.'

Everybody knew about his book, that is, everybody but me, thought Stephanie. And, it seemed, Eleni knew her reason for being back in Crete. Had she been so transparent?

'I'll make you a cup of tea,' Eleni went on, before disappearing into the bar. The hotel cat came to renew its acquaintance with her ankles.

Only now that Eleni had confirmed William was in Chania was Stephanie able to relax. After she'd received the dismaying news of their crossed paths, there had been a rush of telephone calls, first to tell her mother of the change in her plans, then to the airline to re-route her ticket via Athens to Crete.

And all the time, underlying the disappointment of her fruitless trip to London, had been the undeniable possibility that he wouldn't have made the journey to Australia unless he, too, felt they had unfinished business. It made the decision to follow him easy.

Eleni returned with a tea tray — and a dish of sliced cucumber.

'When you've had your tea I want you to go to your room and lie down with cucumber over your eyes,' she instructed. 'That'll put the sparkle back in them.'

Stephanie hadn't believed sleep was possible, but it was late afternoon when she woke. Refreshed, and excited with the thought of seeing William again, she sought out the hotel owner.

'He goes home first, to change, then meets Yanni in the bar before going out to dinner,' explained Eleni.

'Home?'

'Ever since he began writing his book last year he has had a studio in the old town,' she went on. 'Didn't you know?'

A studio in the old town? Stephanie didn't need to ask if it had a blue door, and potted geraniums on the steps, she just knew it did.

The discovery of its existence had revealed her feelings for William on that last day of the tour. Now it seemed she'd been wrong to jump to the conclusion he had a summer love behind that door. It was where he lived. And worked.

But what did that have to do with his feelings for her? Had she been wrong about that, too? Some of her doubts returned.

'Do you want me to give you the address?' Eleni asked. 'I'll draw a map for you.'

'No, thank you, Eleni,' she answered, suddenly unsure. If she was making a mistake, meeting in a public place would take care of any embarrassment.

'I think I'll wait here. I could easily miss him on the way. The crowds, you know.'

The foyer was filling with groups of returning holiday-makers, their faces burned from a day out in the heat. Each time a single figure stepped up to the hotel's glass door and stood silhouetted for a moment against the setting sun, waiting for it to open, Stephanie started up expectantly.

In the end, it was Yanni who arrived first.

There was no doubting his pleasure on seeing her. He strode across the foyer.

'You have come!' he exclaimed, embracing her. 'Good.'

He looked around him. 'We will go into the bar, I think. It will be quieter there.'

Stephanie hesitated, reluctant to leave the sofa by the door, and the safety of numbers. 'William . . . I'll miss . . . '

'No, you will not. He is meeting me in there, and he will come through another door, I promise you, not this one.'

The crowd in the foyer was swelling as he spoke. 'Too many people. Everywhere, too many people,' he added, putting a protective arm at her back.

'Very good for business, Yanni.' Stephanie laughed, allowing herself to be guided into the bar. He was right, it was quieter and, as he said, there was another door on to the street she had forgotten about.

'Now, what will you have to drink?' Yanni asked.

'I was wrong, wasn't I?' he remarked, after ordering for them.

Stephanie searched her memory. 'Wrong about what?'

'The day you both left I told you he would get over it . . . he did not. And because you hid your feelings so well I did not realise it was more than a summer love for you, too.' He leaned forward. 'That is why you are here, I know.'

Before she could answer, Yanni's gaze swung away towards the door. With a raised arm, he signalled their whereabouts. Stephanie turned.

A familiar figure was making his way confidently across the room. She feasted her eyes on the man she had travelled so far to see.

William was almost at their table when he recognised her. There was one unguarded moment of amazement before his English reserve made him careful. And something else.

It was enough. She knew she'd been right to come.

Yanni stood up, a wide smile on his face as he shook William's hand. 'I have work to do,' he said, nodding to both of them. 'We will meet later at Antigone for dinner and we will dance, yes?'

Stephanie hardly heard him, her whole being centred on the man joining her. William reached for her hand and, for a brief moment, gripped it in his.

'Stephanie!' was all he said.

There was a long silence between

them as each searched the other's face.

'How did you know I was here?' William asked at last.

'When I learned I had missed you in England and that you'd gone to Australia, I rang my mother.' Worried that might sound to be presuming too much, Stephanie added, 'Just in case you'd turned up there.'

William raised a quizzical eyebrow. 'And where else would I have gone in Australia?'

'Well, for all I knew, you could have been consulting your publisher. I hear you're writing a book.'

He shook his head. 'My publisher is in England.'

She had a momentary loss of concentration as a teasing thought popped into her head. 'Or,' she continued, 'You could have gone to see Harriet and Sue.'

The look on his face told Stephanie he didn't appreciate her joke.

'Harriet didn't report me after all,' she hastened to add. 'I think you frightened her.'

With a wave of his hand he dismissed the Pearsons as being unworthy of discussion.

'There was someone at your mother's. Is he important?'

A little surprised by his directness, Stephanie shook her head. 'He never was,' she answered. She didn't mean to belittle Martin, but knew she'd never have felt the compulsion to travel halfway across the world to be with him that she had with this man.

The answer seemed to satisfy William. He nodded absently. She wondered if he'd known that all along. But clearly something else was bothering him.

'You didn't tell your parents about me.' There was a slightly accusing tone to his voice. As if he was hurt.

'You didn't tell yours about me,' Stephanie countered defensively.

'I wasn't sure there was any point.'

'Well, I wasn't sure either.'

'I liked them.'

'I liked your mother and father, too.'

'Well, that's settled,' he said drily, his

face clearing. 'Now, what about me?'

'Sorry?'

'How do you feel about me?'

'That's what I've come to find out,' she replied, with growing confidence.

The bar was no longer the refuge it had been earlier; the holiday-makers had found it. William looked up as the spare chair at their table was dragged away to augment a larger group. He brought his gaze back to her and smiled.

'Well, you won't find out sitting in here, will you?' It was more of a statement than a question. Stephanie accepted the challenge. She rose and took his outstretched hand.

15

Outside in the velvety-soft evening air, it seemed natural to leave it there as they walked away into the quietness. Nothing was said.

Stephanie was glad; it was enough that they were together, and all the pieces of the puzzle had fallen into place.

They reached the steps that led up on to the breakwater. William's grip tightened, bringing her to a standstill. Just as naturally, she turned and slipped into his waiting arms.

'I've dreamed of doing this ever since Athens Airport,' he murmured. His lips moved with butterfly-lightness from her forehead to her eyes, alighting briefly on the tip of her nose, then down her cheek until they found the corner of her mouth. But he didn't kiss her; it seemed he had more he wanted to say.

'I don't mean the last day,' he said,

his lips hardly leaving her face. 'Since before that, really.'

Stephanie stirred herself out of her state of near-bliss to ask, 'Before that?'

'The first day, when you ... when you couldn't get your suitcase off the carousel, but you weren't going to give up.' He paused. 'And on the mountain ... you were so ... you had such a good attitude ... I just wanted to kiss you. Badly.'

'I didn't know,' she mumbled, wishing he would stop talking. There would be time enough for that later.

'Because it wasn't the right thing then, I couldn't show it, could I?'

Stephanie became impatient; she had been dreaming, too, though not for as long, and the promise of his lips, so tantalisingly close to hers, had become a torment. 'Perhaps you could show me now,' she suggested.

She felt his grin in the brief moment before he acted on her advice. She thought again of their first, snatched kiss when a cabin-bag and her business satchel had come between them.

Now there was nothing to stop her winding her arms around his neck and kissing him back. And no-one to interrupt.

'It's true what they say,' she murmured contentedly after a while. 'Journeys do end in lovers' meetings.'

'Does that mean what I think it does?'

'Yes, of course,' she replied, thinking that their journeys were proof enough of their feelings for each other. 'But it doesn't happen for summer lovers,' she continued when William let her. 'That's what's so sad about them; they never meet again.'

He held her at arms-length from him, his face serious. 'You understand this is not a summer love, don't you? It's an all-seasons love as far as I'm concerned.'

'We wouldn't have met again if it wasn't, would we?'

Stephanie's perfectly logical answer pleased William. With a whoop of delight he swept her back into his embrace.

We do hope that you have enjoyed reading this large print book.

Did you know that all of our titles are available for purchase?

We publish a wide range of high quality large print books including:
Romances, Mysteries, Classics
General Fiction
Non Fiction and Westerns

Special interest titles available in large print are:
The Little Oxford Dictionary
Music Book, Song Book
Hymn Book, Service Book

Also available from us courtesy of Oxford University Press:
Young Readers' Dictionary
(large print edition)
Young Readers' Thesaurus
(large print edition)

For further information or a free brochure, please contact us at:
Ulverscroft Large Print Books Ltd.,
The Green, Bradgate Road, Anstey,
Leicester, LE7 7FU, England.
Tel: (00 44) **0116 236 4325**
Fax: (00 44) **0116 234 0205**

ELUSIVE LOVE

Karen Abbott

Amelia has always been determined to marry for love . . . but with her elder brother dead and posthumously branded as a traitor, Amelia and her sister find themselves penniless and ostracised by society. When a relative contrives to put an *'eligible parti'* under an obligation to make Amelia an offer, Amelia has to decide whether or not to stand by her principles . . . and face the consequences of turning down what might be her only chance to escape her unbearable situation.

MARRIED TO THE ENEMY

Sheila Holroyd

Faced with the choice of death or marriage to a stranger, Kate marries Lord Alvedon, the powerful servant of Queen Elizabeth. Taken away from everything she has ever known Kate finds it difficult to adjust to the strange new world of Elizabeth's court. Her innocence not only threatens her marriage, it puts her in great danger — and, unknown to her or her husband, a secret enemy plans to kill both of them . . .

TABITHA'S TRIALS

Valerie Holmes

Tabitha is reluctantly released from St Mary's Establishment for Impoverished Girls because Miss Grimley will not break the rules and allow her to remain. She must go into service, contributing to the school so that other girls will benefit. Tabitha rides on the back of a wagon and watches her past drift into the distance. With a heavy heart, she contemplates years of hard work and predictability stretching before her, little realising just what the future has to offer . . .

GENTLEMEN PREFER . . . BRUNETTES

Liz Fielding

Nick Jefferson can't resist a challenge, or a blonde! So when the latest platinum-haired woman to cross his path challenges him to cook her a romantic dinner, he accepts. Unfortunately Nick could burn water . . . Chef Cassie Cornwell is *not* Nick's type — she's a brunette, and the only woman to turn Nick down. She's disappointed he wants her to prepare a seduction feast rather than to share one. Unless Cassie can persuade him that blondes aren't necessarily more fun . . .

THE HONEY TREE

Glenis Wilson

Sparks fly when Merri Williams meets Walt Lime. She's struggling to keep Aunt Prue's riding stables afloat whilst Prue and Walt's Uncle Matt are in Dubai. To avoid bankruptcy, Merri buys more ponies and gives riding lessons to disabled children. But Walt is intent on stopping her. What is he concealing? And why has Prue gone to Dubai? 'When I return I'll tell you — until then you'll be on your own — promise you'll ask Walt for help . . . '

A SUBTLE DECEIT

Anne Hewland

Two eligible gentlemen bring Nerissa Cleveland news of her father's death in Egypt — the unassuming Bernard Martin and the darkly abrupt Lord Brook. Both offer to help her to deal with Giles Cleveland's collection of antiquities — which now seems to be at risk from intruders. The neglected house and grounds hold many secrets . . . but who will assist Nerissa in unravelling the mysteries? Does one of her suitors have sinister motives . . . ? And who will gain her love?